NIGHT MOVES

Other books by Cynthia Danielewski:

Realm of Darkness
Dead of Night
After Dark
Edge of Night

NIGHT MOVES

•

Cynthia Danielewski

AVALON BOOKS
NEW YORK

Published by Thomas Bouregy & Co., Inc.
160 Madison Avenue, New York, NY 10016

Library of Congress Cataloging-in-Publication Data

Danielewski, Cynthia.
  Night moves / Cynthia Danielewski.
      p. cm.
  ISBN 978-0-8034-9818-1 (acid-free paper)
  I. Title.

PS3604.A528N54 2007
813'.6—dc22

                                      2006034821

PRINTED IN THE UNITED STATES OF AMERICA
ON ACID-FREE PAPER
BY HADDON CRAFTSMEN, BLOOMSBURG, PENNSYLVANIA

For Phil and Shirlee Schmelter

Chapter One

The Fourth of July neighborhood block party was winding down as New York Police Detective Jack Reeves rocked his infant son, John, to sleep. Standing on the front porch of his house, he gently patted the baby's back as his head rested on his shoulder, and he glanced around at his neighbors, observing how they were getting their lawn chairs set up by the side of the road to watch the impressive display of fireworks that would be set off over the lake not far from the house. The night air was warm and humid, and the lingering smell of barbecues mingled with the excited sounds of children's voices and the bursting of firecrackers as everybody waited impatiently for the big event to start.

As Jack's eyes scanned the activity going on around him, he caught sight of his wife, Ashley, as she spoke quietly to one of the neighbors. He slowly made his way down the porch steps and over to where she stood.

"How's John?" Ashley asked softly as soon as he

1

reached her side, her hand reaching up to gently touch the baby's black hair, a feature he inherited from his father.

Jack placed a light kiss against his son's head and smiled slightly, the action softening the long scar that ran from his temple to his mouth, a souvenir he carried from his first case in the homicide division of the police force well over a decade ago. "He's out like a light. Do me a favor and fix the blankets in the portable crib so that I can put him down."

"He's only going to get up again once the fireworks start," she warned, moving to the small crib set up by the picnic area to perform the task.

"Probably," Jack agreed as he carefully laid the baby down. "But at least he'll get a little rest."

"Which I guess we should be grateful for," Ashley murmured, thinking of all the long, sleepless nights they had spent since their son came into the world. John was a night baby, there was no disputing that. It had been obvious since the day he was born. But what was also obvious was that the baby had Jack wrapped around his little finger. One small cry was all it took for the normally cynical, conservative, no-nonsense detective to come running. Today had been no exception. While Ashley had spent the afternoon socializing with their neighbors, Jack had spent most of it entertaining their son. And while she would have loved for Jack to get more involved with their community, she wouldn't trade the time he gave John for anything. The man loved his son. Anybody who watched them together knew that.

Jack adjusted the little sleeper that John wore before rising to his full height and running a careless hand through his short strands of dark hair that was showing signs of gray. He glanced at both Ashley and the neighbor she was speaking with, Kayla Smythe. "What were you and Kayla discussing so ardently when I interrupted?"

Ashley reached for a light blanket to cover the baby before responding. "Kayla was just telling me about Richard's big promotion."

Jack turned his head to smile at Kayla, a petite black-haired woman who always seemed to remind him of a pixie. Her close-cropped hair, her small upturned nose and slightly pointed chin all bolstered that impression. She had befriended Ashley as soon as she and her husband, Richard, had moved into the neighborhood, and had even offered to babysit for them if they ever needed it. And though Jack hadn't spent much time with Kayla personally, he knew Ashley appreciated both her friendship and the gesture. "Promotion? I guess congratulations are in order."

Kayla returned his smile. "Thanks. Richard was promoted to Vice President at his brokerage firm. It means longer hours, but it's a great opportunity."

"I wish him luck," Jack said, turning to try and catch sight of the woman's husband. "Where is he, by the way? I haven't seen him all day."

"He went inside to make a phone call a little while ago. He should be out shortly," she replied just as several roman candles blasted into the night sky in a kaleidoscope of colors, causing the neighborhood children to shriek with excitement.

Jack automatically reached down to soothe the baby as he stirred. "It looks like the fireworks show is starting."

"Yeah. I'd better go and let Richard know. I'm sure

he doesn't want to miss this. I'll be right back," Kayla said, turning to walk across the street to her house.

Ashley watched her leave. "She seems excited about Richard's promotion."

"That's understandable. Richard works hard. I'm sure they've both been waiting for some kind of acknowledgment of his efforts."

"I've noticed him arriving home after midnight lately. When you put those type of hours in, you're entitled to something," Ashley agreed, moving over to take a seat in the lawn chair next to the crib.

Jack smiled at Ashley's words and reached out to tenderly move a strand of her blond hair away from her eyes, thinking about how beautiful she looked. Already tan from the summer sun, she also sported a new hairstyle that fell just below her shoulders and was angled toward her face, highlighting her features and bringing attention to the rich brown color of her eyes. But as he looked at her, he couldn't help but think that she was ready for the night to end. He really wasn't surprised. She had been running at full steam all week.

"How are you holding up?" he asked with a change of subject, his concern for her well-being uppermost in his mind. Ashley barely slept at night with their son's schedule, and yet she had been the one who had suggested the block party, the one who did all the legwork to put it together. He knew she had to be tired. He was exhausted just watching her. She had gone out of her way that day to make sure that all of the neighbors participating in the event felt like they made a contribution to the day. And in reality they did. But it was Ashley's organizational skills that ensured everything came together without a hitch. It was Ashley's relentless drive that brought the community together. Those attributes served her well in her job as a reporter, and it was those qualities that made her so good at accomplishing whatever task she tackled. And while Jack admired her for her tenaciousness, gatherings like this were never his style. He preferred quiet nights spent with just her and the baby.

"Good. But I have to admit, I'm glad today is almost over. I never realized how much work was involved in organizing a block party."

"Maybe next year, you'll let someone else take the reins."

"Maybe," she murmured ambiguously, motioning to the empty chair beside her. "Sit with me."

"Sure," Jack replied, moving over to join her.

He was just about to sit down when a loud succession of exploding firecrackers filled the night, followed by the distinct sound of a gunshot. He stiffened, his eyes looking toward the sprawling modern ranch house across the street, the area where the shot was fired.

"That sounded like it came from Kayla and Richard's house," Ashley said with alarm as she quickly got to her feet. She automatically reached for the baby and held him protectively against her.

"Yeah, it did. Get the baby into the house," Jack ordered. "I'm going to see what's going on."

Ashley did as he instructed, but she couldn't stop from turning and watching with concern as he rushed to their neighbors' house.

Jack forced his way through the small group of people that were gathering on the front lawn, identifying himself as a police officer while he ordered them to step off the property. The action was instinctive.

Regardless of whether or not anybody was injured by the gunshot, he wanted the area cleared. He wasn't willing to take any risks when it came to people's safety.

He didn't bother with formalities when he arrived at Richard and Kayla's door; instead he reached for the doorknob, his only thought to get inside the house to make sure everybody was all right. Finding it locked, he banged his fist against the door and shouted, "Kayla! Richard!"

When there was no response, he took a step back and, placing his foot against the door panel, he kicked the door in. Total silence greeted him.

Entering the foyer, he paused for a moment, his hand automatically going to the gun that was always strapped to his waist. Pulling the firearm out of the holster, he listened intently for any sound, while his eyes scanned the expanse of the house's open floor plan, looking for anything out of the ordinary, anything that would explain the gunshot. But the room was seemingly undisturbed. Cautiously, he began searching the other rooms.

The smell of gunpowder was strong in the air as he made his way to the back of the house. Mentally bracing himself, he entered one of the rear bedrooms, but he wasn't totally prepared for the sight that greeted him. Richard Smythe lay on the floor in a pool of blood.

Chapter Two

Jack quickly crossed over to Richard, his eyes automatically searching his still form for any movement, any sign of life. But Richard Smythe's tall, well-toned frame was motionless against the dark tan carpet that was saturated with blood. There was no twitching of facial muscles, no fluttering of his closed eyelids. Jack immediately bent down and felt for a pulse, but he couldn't detect one. Cursing under his breath, he reached for his cell phone and called the police station to report the homicide, while his eyes scanned the room, trying to determine exactly what had happened.

As he glanced around, he noticed the open French doors that led to the backyard. After getting assurance that backup was on the way, he stood and took a step toward the French doors, but stopped when he heard a muffled sound coming from the closet.

He swiftly turned in that direction. Adrenaline flowing, he made his way over to the closet and reached out to jerk the door open, his gun poised and ready to fire. "Freeze! Police!"

Kayla Smythe's tear-drenched, frightened blue eyes looked up to meet his as she sat curled in the corner of the closet, almost in a fetal position. "Jack . . ." she wept, her voice breaking on a fresh sob.

Jack crouched down in front of her, his eyes taking in everything about her appearance, about her demeanor. "What happened?" he demanded, trying to determine if she was injured. He noticed some blood-stains on her shirt, but he couldn't tell if it was her blood.

Kayla didn't respond, she just sat huddled in the corner shuddering with sobs.

"Kayla, are you hurt?" Jack asked, the full range of his senses kicking in as he tried to find out what had happened, while being fully aware of the danger of the situation. He didn't know who shot Richard, or where the perpetrator was. And though he didn't sense another person's presence in the room, only a fool became complacent. On guard for any sort of threat around him, he continued to try and get a response from her. "Kayla, I need you to talk to me. Are you hurt?" he repeated when she just continued to cry uncontrollably.

His words finally got through to her and she shook her head. "Richard . . ." she stammered, bordering on hysteria.

Jack tried to make sense out of what she was saying. Her voice was barely coherent, and she was shaking uncontrollably. Her obvious distress tore at his heart, but he banked down his instinct to offer comfort, knowing that he had to get her to talk. Taking her on her word that she wasn't seriously injured, he reached out and gently grasped her shoulders, forcing her to make eye contact with him, trying to get her to focus. "Kayla! What happened? Who was here?"

"A man," she finally got out, her body heaving with sobs.

"Where?"

When she didn't immediately answer, Jack released his hold on her and jumped to his feet. It was clear that Kayla wasn't in control of her emotions, and he needed to get a handle on what happened. He needed to know if the person that shot Richard was still on the grounds. With a final glance in her direction, he ordered, "Stay here!"

Jack didn't know if she comprehended what he had said, but he also knew he couldn't afford to let valuable time slip away. Keeping his guard up, he checked out the rest of the bedroom before moving to the French doors and stepping into the dark backyard.

As he walked out onto a small patio, the space was immediately illuminated by a sensor security light. He looked up at the fixture briefly before glancing around the area, trying to catch a glimpse of any shadows to determine if anybody was there. But he couldn't detect anything. The air was still, and the only sounds that could be heard were the voices of the neighbors gathered at the front of the house and the ongoing explosion of fireworks.

After doing a quick search of the grounds outside, he made his way back inside and over to the closet. Kayla was still curled up inside. Reaching down, he offered her a hand to help her up, using his own body as a shield as he tried to block her view of her husband's body. "Whoever was here is gone. Come on. Let's get you into the other room," he said, wanting to spare her the trauma of seeing her husband lying in his own blood.

Kayla stared at Jack's hand for a long moment before she finally put her own into it. "Richard . . ." she cried, trying to catch a glimpse of her husband as she let Jack help her from the closet.

Jack quickly turned her away from the scene. "Don't," he warned, escorting her through the hall. He heard the sound of the police sirens as they arrived at the house, and felt some of the tension leave his body at the realization that backup had arrived. He cast a look down at Kayla. "In a moment, this place is going to be swarming with police. Don't panic. I'll take care of everything," he promised, feeling her shuddering against him.

Kayla nodded, taking comfort in his words.

Jack squeezed her hand in reassurance, his gaze automatically going to the front door as he heard footsteps approaching it. Within moments it opened. He immediately caught sight of his police partner, Ryan Parks, walking toward him. Jack wasn't surprised that he was there. Though Ryan had been off duty that night, he was also a dedicated cop. He always had his cell phone with him so that the precinct could communicate with him. Regardless of his laid-back personality, his unconventional appearance of wearing his gray-streaked brown hair long and clubbed in the back, everybody on the police force knew that Ryan was someone you could count on. And the seriousness of his expression at the moment, the way his eyes were focused on Jack, attested to the fact that Ryan had come to the Smythes' house prepared to work.

Jack exchanged a small nod of greeting with Ryan before he looked at the people following in his wake. Directly behind Ryan was the chief of police, Ed Stall, and a small army of officers.

"What happened?" Ed demanded, not bothering with pleasantries. His austere features were more stern than usual, and his pale blue eyes were almost piercing as his eyes flew from Jack and focused on Kayla.

Jack felt Kayla recoil slightly as Ed's attention focused on her, and he knew it was imperative to give the woman some breathing room and a chance to calm down. He didn't want to take any chances that Ed's harsh persona would scare her. Ed could be intimidating without even trying. The stockiness of his frame, the thick thatch of premature gray hair, the bold straight lines of his brow, and the cragginess of his features gave the impression that this was a man you didn't want to cross. And though Jack knew that Ed was an even-tempered, fair-minded man, he was concerned that Kayla wouldn't see him that way. He knew that if she felt threatened, she might not talk. It was a chance he wasn't willing to take. Handing Kayla over to a uniformed officer, he waited for them to walk away before he answered. "Homicide. The body's in the bedroom," he said, turning to lead the way back to the scene of the crime. "The man's name is Richard Smythe. He and his wife, Kayla, own the house."

"Kayla? That's the woman you were with?" Ed asked.

"Yeah. She was in the house when the gun went off,"

Jack replied, stepping into the bedroom with Ryan and Ed at his heels.

Ryan paused for a moment as he entered the bed-room, whistling through his teeth as he saw the amount of blood pooled around the body. Though he was used to seeing the by-product of violence, having worked undercover in the narcotics division before transferring to homicide, there was usually an indication of what led to the loss of someone's life. That wasn't the case in this instance. There was no sign of any struggle, no outward signs that would explain what had occurred. "The dispatcher said you heard the shot?"

Jack nodded and rubbed a weary hand across the back of his neck. "It followed a succession of fire-crackers going off."

"How long before you called the station?" Ed asked as he walked over to the body and crouched down to examine the victim. He noticed that there were no vis-ible bruises on the man's exposed skin.

"It couldn't have been more than five minutes. I was across the street with Ashley when the shot fired. It didn't take me that long to gain access to the house."

"It looks like the guy didn't have a prayer of surviv-ing," Ed said, not looking up from his examination of the deceased.

"No," Jack agreed before motioning around the room. "And there's no sign of any struggle. Either the man was totally surprised by the attack or he knew his murderer," he stated, looking at the pristinely made-up bed, and noticing the lack of any apparent disruption of the articles in the room. Now that he had Kayla out of the room, out of danger, he had an opportunity to fully scrutinize the crime scene. And what he saw bothered him. The room was clean. Too clean. There was absolutely no indication that an intruder had been there.

Ryan performed a quick inspection of the room, noticing the open doors that led outside. He turned to study the body for a moment before he walked over and looked at the door frame. "Did you notice anything? Anyone?" he asked Jack, studying the wood for splintering, anything that would lead him to believe there was a forced entry into the house.

"No. To be honest, I didn't see Richard all day. Kayla was in our yard talking to Ashley when she decided to come over here to get him so that they could watch the fireworks together. After I gained access to the house, I found Kayla in the closet," Jack said.

"Has she said anything?" Ed asked.

"Only that a man was here," Jack replied.

"That's not much," Ryan murmured, continuing to inspect the door frame. "There's no sign of forced entry on this door."

"No, I know. I looked at it briefly before," Jack said, walking over to where Ryan stood before stepping outside. He motioned to the light fixture that illuminated the patio. "This sensor light wasn't on when I arrived. If someone entered or exited the house this way, it should have been. This type of security light usually stays on awhile after being activated."

Ryan joined Jack on the patio, looking at the light and then looking down at the concrete foundation. "The patio is clean. There're no muddy footprints or stray bloodstains."

"So, there's nothing that would lead us to believe that the perpetrator came through that doorway," Ed said, glancing at the opening before looking back down at the victim. "From the position of the body, I think we can rule out that the shot was fired from the yard. It looks like Richard Smythe fell straight back. That would mean that our shooter would have had to come from the master bathroom area or closet."

"Both logical places for somebody to lie in wait," Jack murmured, stepping back inside the bedroom.

Ryan followed him. "Did you notice anyone today enter through the front door of the house? There are a lot of people outside. Is there anybody that you know of that may have had a problem with Richard Smythe?"

"No. But I wasn't watching the house during the day," Jack admitted. "There was too much other stuff going on."

"What about his wife? Are there any marital problems that you know of?" Ryan asked.

Jack shrugged. "If they had a problem, I wasn't aware of it. Kayla had mentioned tonight that her husband just received a promotion at the brokerage firm he worked at. She seemed excited."

"Maybe there's someone at his firm who had a motive to murder the man," Ed suggested.

"Possibly," Jack conceded. "As soon as Kayla calms down a little, I'll talk to her and see what I can find out."

"She's in bad shape. It might take some time to get all the information from her," Ryan said.

Jack sighed and ran a restless hand through his hair. "Yeah, I know. But right now, she's the only one who knows anything about what happened," he said, stepping back as a forensics team came into the bedroom to process the area.

Ryan watched as a photographer started shooting pictures of the body. "How many of your neighbors participated in the block party?"

"Almost everyone. Ashley organized it. I'd have to check with her to see who declined and why," Jack said.

"What time did it start?" Ed asked.

"Officially, about one o'clock. The street barricades went up shortly before that," Jack said.

Ed considered Jack's words and the timeframe they had to work with. "I gave instructions to the officers outside to start interviewing the crowd. I'll call the station and have them arrange for patrol cars to canvas the neighborhood and see if anybody not involved with the party noticed anyone or anything suspicious." He looked at Jack. "Is there anybody else that we should contact for questioning? A disc jockey that was hired? Any party rental places?"

"Yeah, there is. They cleared out about an hour ago, but Ashley has a list with the names, addresses, and phone numbers of who was hired."

"I'll send one of the officers over to your house to get it, and then I'll call the station and get the ball rolling on what needs to be done," Ed said.

Jack gave a slight nod. "I'll call Ashley and let them know they're on their way. She'll be on edge because of what's going on over here."

"I'll call her," Ed offered. "You stay here with Ryan and see if you can come up with anything that might help with the investigation."

"All right. When you call the station, have them run a check to see if there are any guns registered to either Richard or Kayla Smythe at this address," Jack instructed.

Ryan looked at Jack curiously. "You think the weapon used to kill the guy belongs to either him or his wife?"

"I have no idea. It's just something I want ruled out," Jack replied.

"I'll take care of it," Ed promised. "I'll also have them perform a trace metal detection test and a gunpowder residue test on Kayla Smythe so that we can rule her out as the shooter. I'll see about getting her fingerprints at the same time. We'll need them to determine who else may have been in the house."

"Be careful how you approach her with the idea. We don't want to alarm her," Jack said, not wanting to do anything that would prevent Kayla from cooperating with the police. He knew most people immediately went on the defensive when they were questioned. It was just human nature. But the fact was that family members almost always came under suspicion during a homicide investigation, especially when there were no outside witnesses to the crime. The process of eliminating all possible suspects had to be followed regardless of the person's relationship to the victim.

"I'll be my most diplomatic," Ed assured him before stepping away to take care of business.

Ryan looked at Jack as soon as Ed left the room. "This is some way to spend the Fourth."

Jack grunted in agreement and glanced at his watch. "Were you at the station when I called? You two got here quick."

"No. I ran into Ed down by the lake. I took Jane there to watch the fireworks after her parents' barbecue," Ryan replied, referring to his girlfriend.

"She must have loved that you had to rush off."

Ryan smiled slightly at Jack's comment. "Jane understands the demands of my job," he said as he looked around at the orderliness of the bedroom. "Everything in this room looks like it has a place," he observed, walking around the area, noticing the careful placement of the knickknacks on the glistening cherry wood furniture, the crispness of the linens on the bed.

"Yeah, it does," Jack agreed. "There's absolutely no evidence to support that this was the result of a robbery."

"If I had to make a guess, I would say that this was a premeditated act," Ryan told him.

"I'm getting that impression too," Jack said, reaching for a pair of latex gloves from one of the cases the forensics team brought and pulling them on.

"What was your initial thought when you walked in?"

"That there was somebody else here. But there's no evidence to suggest that. At least not in this room," Jack replied just as Ed came back into the room.

"Okay, everything's set. The patrol cars are on the way, and I spoke to the officers outside. The property has been secured and a couple of them are on their way over to your house to see about getting the list from Ashley," Ed said, reaching for his own pair of gloves.

"How's Ashley doing?" Jack asked.

"She's concerned for Kayla. She offered to talk to her if we need her to," Ed informed him.

Jack nodded, knowing that he wouldn't take her up on her offer, at least not tonight. The case was too new, too raw. And he had nothing that exonerated Kayla from being involved in this mess. There was no way that he would subject his family to any sort of danger. "What about your call to the station? Did they come up with any guns registered to either Richard or Kayla Smythe?"

Ed expelled a small sigh. "No."

"It was worth checking," Jack said, crouching down to search the area underneath the bed for possible evidence. When he was through, he stood, his fingers gingerly holding a bullet casing.

Ryan studied the casing held between Jack's fingertips, not surprised by the find. "You only found one?" he asked, reaching for a small evidence bag so that Jack could preserve and tag the evidence.

"Just one," Jack confirmed, dropping the item into the bag and sealing the bag closed.

"If it came from the gun used to shoot Richard Smythe, it could be that our killer kicked it under the bed when they attempted to get out of the room," Ryan said, theorizing aloud.

"And if that happened, he would have turned in the direction of the doorway that leads into the hallway," Ed murmured.

Jack glanced at the doorway in question, his eyes skimming past the closet where he had found Kayla before looking at Ed. "What was Kayla's response to the gunpowder residue test and giving her fingerprints?"

"She's willing to cooperate. But I have to be honest, I think the lady is in severe shock. According to one of the officers with her, she was violently ill just a little while ago."

Jack frowned. "Is she okay now?"

"For the moment, but she's not that coherent. The officer with her is trying to get a description of the suspect so that we can get out an APB, but he's not having much luck."

"If he has no success, I'll talk to her," Jack offered, handing his find to one of the forensic experts who was searching the room. He watched as the dresser in the bedroom was thoroughly dusted for fingerprints before glancing once more at Ed. "Did you talk to the coroner's office?"

"Yeah. They should be here shortly."

"Good. Once the body's removed, we'll have more room to maneuver," Jack said as he moved over to the closet where he found Kayla. Bending down, he began searching the area.

"What are you looking for?" Ryan asked, walking up beside Jack.

"I'm not sure. Kayla was leaning toward the back wall when I found her. Maybe there's something in here that will shed some light on what happened," Jack said without looking up. "Hand me a flashlight, will you?"

"Sure," Ryan replied, moving off to get the item. He was back within moments. "Here."

"Thanks," Jack said, shining the light against the walls, looking for any blood streaks.

While Jack searched the closet, Ryan looked at the clothes hanging from the rod, the shoes and purses that lined an upper shelf. "This closet looks like it belongs to the wife," he said, noticing the dresses and skirts that filled up the space. There was no sign of any clothes belonging to a man. Taking a step back, he reached for his own pair of gloves and pulled them on before walking over to the dresser that was being dusted for prints. He began opening the drawers and searching the contents, and he was surprised to find that all of the possessions appeared to belong to a woman. His forehead creased in a frown, he quickly walked over to search the armoire and night tables, only to find the same thing. "This is strange."

Jack looked up from his task and over at Ryan. "What is?"

"From all indications, this is the master bedroom. But there's no sign of any items belonging to a man," Ryan said.

"At all?" Ed questioned, moving over to where Ryan stood so that he could see for himself.

Ryan took a step back as Ed approached, allowing him access to the area. "Not unless you see something that I'm missing."

Ed performed his own search, confirming what Ryan said. He turned to face Jack. "Ryan's right. There's no indication that a man shared this room. You had mentioned earlier that you didn't think there were marital problems. But maybe there were," he suggested.

Jack gave a slight shrug. "It's possible. I don't really know them that well. And Ashley did mention in passing that the guy has been working long hours. We'll have to question Kayla on it when we talk to her," he said, turning back to finish searching the closet.

Ryan watched Jack's actions. "Anything in there?"

"I'm not sure. Hand me one of the small evidence bags and a pair of tweezers," Jack murmured as he noticed a reflection of light bounce off an object on the floor when the beam from the flashlight hit it.

Ryan did as he requested. "Sure."

Jack took the bag from Ryan. "Thanks," he said, carefully transferring the object into it.

Ed waited impatiently while Jack performed the task. "Well? What did you find?"

Jack held the clear plastic bag up to the light and showed them the contents. "A button."

Ryan moved forward to get a better look. "I'm not sure if a button being found in the closet is so unusual."

"True," Jack said as he walked back to where Richard Smythe's body lay on the floor. He crouched down next to him. "But if it matches the ones on our victim's shirt, it may just be a clue."

"Well?" Ed prompted after a long pause of silence.

"We have a match."

Chapter Three

"There are a lot of things that could explain the button in the closet," Ryan said, reaching out to take the bag from Jack so that he could examine the object. "It's a fairly common pattern. Maybe it belongs to another article of clothing."

"The thread attached to the back matches Richard Smythe's shirt color. And as you pointed out, it doesn't look like any of his clothes are in the closet," Jack replied, glancing at the evidence.

"There's a slim chance that the button was on the floor before tonight," Ed reminded him.

"Yeah, there is," Jack agreed. "But I would have a hard time buying that. I didn't know Richard well, but any time I did see him, he was always impeccably dressed. I can't imagine him wearing a shirt that was missing a button."

"Maybe because of the holiday he was less concerned about his appearance today," Ryan suggested.

"That's doubtful," Jack answered, thinking back to all the times he had seen Richard. The man always looked as if he had just stepped out of the pages of a style magazine.

Ryan lifted his shoulder slightly. "You know the man better than us. Unless something indicates otherwise, we'll go on the assumption that the button ended up in the closet after the shooting tonight," he said, handing the item in question back to Jack.

Jack looked at it once more before handing it over to one of the technicians to log. "This leaves us with one problem."

"What's that?" Ed asked.

"The button was in the closet where I found Kayla. It would make sense that she had something to do with it ending up in there," Jack replied.

Ed's eyes met Jack's. "There could be another explanation for it."

"What?"

"The closet's in the same direction as the doorway. It's possible that the person who shot Richard—the person who kicked the bullet casing under the bed—came to the closet instead of going into the hallway," Ed replied.

"Captain Stall?" a uniformed officer called from the doorway, interrupting the conversation of the three men.

Ed turned to look at the officer. "Yes?"

"We found an open window in the basement," the officer informed him.

Ed turned to look at Jack and Ryan. "This may be the clue we've been waiting for to explain how Richard Smythe's killer entered or left the house. Let's go see what we have."

The three of them followed the officer down the short hallway to the basement door located off the kitchen. The search going on in the residence had encompassed every room, and they were forced to step aside as bags of evidence were carried through the rooms and to the front door.

The officer looked back at them before he descended the steps into the basement. "A few of these stairs don't feel too steady. Be careful where you step."

"Thanks for the warning," Ed murmured, following the officer down the wooden steps and into the unfinished basement, which was currently overrun with officers and technicians involved in the search. He glanced back once to make sure that Jack and Ryan were close behind.

Jack looked around the area that was illuminated by several high-power beam lights that had been set up to assist with the evidence search. He observed the activity going on around them, the diligent actions of those taking part in the search. Watching as possible evidence was gathered, he couldn't help but notice the cobwebs that took over practically every corner and crevice in the area, the water stains that lined the cement walls. The dampness in the room was a tangible force, and a strong musty odor permeated the air. As he glanced around and took everything in, he came to the realization that the space was rarely used by the occupants of the home, at least for living purposes. "From the condition of this place, it doesn't like either Richard or Kayla spent any real time down here," he said, speaking his thoughts aloud.

"Which doesn't explain why the window would be

open. Either one of them opened it, or the person that killed Richard did," Ryan said.

Jack looked at the height of the window and he realized that if someone wanted to use the window as an exit, in all likelihood, they would need something to stand on, something that would give them the leverage they needed to get through the opening. He glanced around to see if he could find anything that would support the weight of a man. There was nothing. The items near the window looked too flimsy for the task.

He looked back at the window, gauging the dimensions of the opening. He was trying to determine if somebody would have been able to hoist themselves up to the windowsill so that they could escape. He came to the conclusion that it was possible. Not easy, but definitely possible, especially if the person had upper-body strength. "The space is tight, but it's large enough for an adult to fit through."

Ryan grunted in agreement. "It would be a lot easier for someone to get into the basement than out, though."

The technician who was dusting the area for fingerprints stepped back as soon as he finished the task. "There are a few clear prints."

Ed nodded, and studied the other windows in the basement, which were all closed. "This window faces the rear of the yard, on the opposite side of the house from where the bedroom is located. If somebody left this way, the chances of anybody noticing would have been slim." He turned to look at Jack. "You had mentioned that the security light wasn't on in the patio area off the bedroom. This is far enough away from there so that the sensor wouldn't have been triggered if someone left the house this way."

"That's true," Ryan agreed. "And from the looks of things when we arrived, most of the neighbors were on their front lawns. I doubt any one of them would have noticed somebody running through the yard over here."

"Yeah, but there are a lot of kids in the neighborhood, and they were all over the place playing. It's possible one of them might have noticed something suspicious," Jack said.

"We'll know more after we get done interviewing everybody," Ed said.

Jack studied the other items housed in the basement, noticing the old crates and boxes that lined one wall, and the suitcases resting in a corner. None of them looked sturdy enough to support someone's weight, but the items did give an indication of what the basement was used for. "This place looks like it's used strictly as a storage area. If someone used the window to get in and out of the house, they could have been waiting down here awhile before they decided to make their way upstairs."

"Meaning?" Ryan prompted.

"With all the stuff down here, it's possible that the intruder would have been able to hide down here, even if Richard or Kayla came into the basement," Jack replied.

"Undetected," Ryan murmured, thinking about Jack's words.

"That's right. And if you think about it, Richard's killer hanging out down here makes sense. There're a lot of kids in the neighborhood that get up early to play outside. I'm not sure that someone would take a chance on being spotted in the daylight hours. There's a strong possibility that someone came into the house during the night, and waited for the right moment to make their move. There would have been less of a chance of being noticed."

"That would suggest that our perpetrator was familiar with the neighborhood," Ed said.

"With the little amount we know so far, I would say that's a safe assumption. This whole thing is just too clean. I mean, think about it. Other than this open window, nothing else seems to be disturbed," Jack said.

"We'll need to talk to Kayla before we can confirm that," Ed pointed out.

"Which we should be doing shortly," Jack murmured, looking at his watch. "The coroner should be arriving any minute. I'm going to head back upstairs to see if he's here."

"I'll go with you," Ed said before shooting a glance at Ryan. "Stay here and see if anything shows?"

"You got it," Ryan replied.

"Thanks," Ed replied, turning to lead the way back up the staircase. "We'll call you if we find out anything."

Chapter Four

An hour later, the body had been removed, and Jack and Ryan sat across from Kayla Smythe in the living room as she drank deeply from a bottle of water in an effort to compose herself. The officer that had been speaking to her before had no luck in getting a decent description from her on the man she saw kill Richard. In fact, he had only succeeded in upsetting her. So Jack was going to see if he could coax the information from her. He was hoping that her familiarity with him might enable her to relax enough so that she could concentrate on what she witnessed.

Jack glanced briefly at Roger Paget, a sketch artist with the police department who sat quietly on the sidelines waiting for the interview to start, before his gaze shifted to the search of the house that was still going on. He caught sight of the ever-growing crowd outside as an officer opened the front door so that bags of evidence could be stored in the police van parked on the driveway. The spectators were lining the street as the police kept them off the property, and the flashbulbs going off outside were an indication that the Press had a strong presence there tonight.

Jack studied the activity only briefly before he forced his attention back to the woman who sat before him. Though he noticed that Kayla had calmed down slightly, she was still shaky. She had placed her water bottle onto an end table, and she sat there quietly, her hands trembling uncontrollably where they rested on her lap. She stared at him with wide, frightened eyes.

"I know this is tough on you, Kayla, but I need to find out what happened here tonight," Jack began, leaning forward in his chair slightly as he tried to make some sort of connection with the woman; as he tried to gain her trust. Though she had lived across the street from him for well over a year, Jack really didn't know her that well. Ashley was the one that had befriended her. He didn't know what Kayla's normal demeanor was, or how she behaved in a crisis. He had no real former knowledge to draw from to determine if she was being truthful with him, or if she was trying to cover up something. He knew he needed to get a general reading on her, and he knew he needed to do it fast.

Kayla took a shuddering breath and nodded in understanding. She reached for her water and took another sip before speaking. "I'll try and answer your questions," she murmured, visibly trying to get a grip on her emotions.

"I appreciate that," Jack told her gently. "And if you need to stop at any point, you just let me know."

"Okay," she said, shifting slightly on the sofa.

Jack watched her actions. She was nervous, that

much he could tell. But he also knew her reaction was normal. Almost everybody experienced some apprehension when dealing with the police. "Why don't you start by telling us what happened here tonight."

At his question, her eyes teared up. She took a few moments to collect her thoughts before she began. "I came in to get Richard so that we could watch the fireworks together . . ." she said, her voice trailing off.

"And?" he prompted gently when it didn't look like she would continue. He noticed the vacant look that came into her eyes as if she was no longer aware of her surroundings. He knew without being told that she was reliving the events that had transpired that night. And he also knew that was just human nature. Only the most cold-blooded of people would be able to get through the interview process without having flashbacks. His instincts told him that Kayla didn't fit into that category. Knowing that the interview was traumatic for her, he was careful to keep his voice soft so that he wouldn't add to her distress. He needed to get her to open up. He needed answers. He couldn't afford to put her on the defensive.

Kayla took a deep shuddering breath. "I didn't see Richard when I came into the house," she said after a long pause, reaching up to wipe tears away from her eyes with her fingertips.

Jack automatically reached for his handkerchief and handed it to her. "Take your time," he said, waiting patiently for her to compose herself.

"I'm sorry," she whispered.

"Don't be. You're doing fine," Jack assured her.

"This is so hard," she murmured, her voice choking on a sob.

"I know," Jack acknowledged. "And if it was something that could wait, I wouldn't put you through this."

She nodded, accepting the truth in his words. Taking another deep breath, she continued. "When I came into the house, I heard a noise coming from the back bedrooms."

"What kind of noise?" Ryan asked.

She looked startled by the question. "What?"

"What did the noise sound like? Footsteps, shuffling, banging?" Jack quickly clarified, not wanting her to get distracted.

Kayla's eyes met Jack's briefly before she admitted, "I'm not sure how to categorize it. I just knew someone was in the back of the house. I thought it was Richard walking around."

"Did you say anything at that point?" Ryan asked.

"I called Richard's name, but he didn't answer. So I went back to get him," she said, her hands anxiously twisting the handkerchief she held. "I was walking into the bedroom when I saw him."

"Saw who?" Jack questioned.

"A man. He was holding Richard at gunpoint. He was talking in a low voice. He was angry. He seemed to be blaming my husband for something."

"Did Richard say anything in response?" Jack asked, curious if she would be able to confirm if Richard knew his killer.

"Not while I was there."

"Have you ever seen the man before?" Jack asked.

"No," she replied.

"Are you positive?" Jack persisted, studying her movements, her facial expression for any indication that she was being less than truthful.

"Not one hundred percent. Everything happened so quickly," she said, her tone of voice rising an octave.

Jack sensed the panic that was on the verge of overtaking her, and he quickly set out to try and reassure her. "You're doing fine, Kayla."

She wiped away some more tears. "I want to help."

"I know you do," Jack assured her. "I have a few more question, and then we'll get down to the basics. When you came into the house, did you notice anything out of place? Anything missing?"

"No."

"How about when you saw the man talking to Richard? Did you notice him carrying anything? Something that would make you think he came here to rob your house?" Jack asked.

"I just saw the gun," she said softly, paling at the image that she evoked.

Jack didn't miss her reaction. "I know it's hard, but try not to dwell on that. I need you to concentrate on what the man looked like. I need a description of him. Could you make a guess at his age?"

"He looked about Richard's height—six foot, average build. I would say he looked to be in his early forties."

"What color hair?" Ryan asked.

"I don't know. He had a dark cap on. It looked like a ski cap."

"You couldn't see any of his hair? Maybe in a place that the hat didn't reach?" Ryan asked.

"Not that I noticed. He had a heavy beard though. It was black. It almost looked dyed."

Jack looked at her curiously. "What makes you say that?"

"It was too dark. It didn't seem natural."

"How about his eyes? Did you notice the color?" Jack asked.

"They were brown. Bloodshot. They looked irritated," she recalled.

Jack frowned at the description. "Irritated in what way? Like he was drinking? On drugs?"

She shook her head slightly. "No. They looked the way some people's do when they wear contact lenses."

"What about his facial features? Anything distinguishing? Any scars or birthmarks?" Jack asked.

"Not that I recall. But to be honest, I can't be sure. Some of his features seem so clear in my mind, and others are just a blur," she said, choking on the words.

"That's normal," Jack assured her. "You just had a major shock. Don't get upset if you don't recall something. If you remember anything later, you can always call me. You have my home phone number. But for the moment, try and concentrate on what you saw when you walked into the room. The features of the man that you can remember. Was there anything that stood out that you could describe? His lips, his cheekbones, his nose?"

"There was something about his nose. It may have been broken at one time. There was a bump on the bridge," she said, her finger unconsciously tracing the area on her own nose as she spoke.

"Is there anything else that you can remember about his face?" Jack asked, giving her time to think. He didn't want to rush her. It was important that she be as detailed as possible with what she could recall.

"There was nothing else that stood out. Nothing that I remember. The knit hat he was wearing covered most of his forehead."

"What about his clothes? What did he have on?" Ryan asked, casting a quick look at the sketch artist, and noticing that his pencil was flying across the paper.

"I'm not sure. I just know it was something black."

Ryan raised an eyebrow. "Long sleeve? Short sleeve?"

"Long," she said with a frown. "I think it was some sort of pullover. I didn't notice any buttons or zipper."

"How about gloves? Was he wearing a pair?" Ryan asked.

"Yes. They were black. That I'm sure of."

Jack gave her a look of encouragement. "You had mentioned that you heard him talking when you got to the bedroom. Did you hear what he said? Did he have an accent? A drawl?" he questioned in an attempt to find out as much information as he could. The description she was giving was sketchy, minimal at best. All of the characteristics she was describing would be easy enough for someone to change; easy enough for somebody to mask. He needed something concrete to work with. Something that would enable them to narrow down the search for a suspect.

Kayla took a deep breath before responding. "I couldn't make out any of the words. I just know he was angry. It seemed as if he came here to confront Richard about something."

"But you have no idea what?" Jack asked.

"No."

Jack thought she might expand on the comment, but she didn't. After a brief pause, he pressed on with the interview. "Did Richard have any enemies that you were aware of? Anybody who may have held a grudge against him for any reason? Or against you for that matter?"

There was a slight pause before she answered. "No." '

Jack noticed that she stilled briefly at the question. Though it was only for a moment, he couldn't help but wonder if she was possibly holding back information. "You seemed to hesitate a little bit with your response. Are you sure that Richard didn't have any problems with anybody? Did anybody make any threats against him?"

She was quiet for a long moment before she admitted, "There was one instance, but I don't know if it means anything."

"What was it?" Jack asked.

"Richard was involved in a car accident a few months ago. It was late at night, and he was stopped at a red light. A truck rear-ended him. The driver of the other vehicle claimed that Richard had braked suddenly. He accused him of deliberately trying to cause the accident."

Jack's eyes narrowed at her comment. "Did Richard ever mention why the man accused him of that? Did the other driver give any indication for the reason behind his remark?"

"He said the man accused him of cutting him off while he was driving. Richard denied it."

"How long ago was this?" Jack asked.

"April or May. I can't be sure."

"Do you remember the name of the other driver?" Jack asked.

"No."

"Was an accident report filed?" Ryan asked.

"I think so. Richard handled everything with the insurance company, so I never actually saw any of the paperwork."

"If there's a report, we should be able to look into it," Jack assured her, knowing that he could obtain the information through the background check. He stared at her briefly before continuing, trying to gauge her frame of mind. He knew that his next question would be hard for her. "Tell me, what did you do when you saw the man holding Richard at gunpoint?"

She shrugged helplessly and her tears began to flow freely as she was forced once more to relive the moment. "I panicked. I must have made some kind of sound because when the man turned to look at me, Richard grabbed the gun. They struggled for a moment and the gun fired. Richard fell immediately."

Jack steeled himself against her tears, against offering any sympathy at this point. He didn't want to sidetrack her. "What happened then?"

Her eyes met his, wide and frightened. "The man came toward me. I thought he was going to kill me. He actually reached for me, but something distracted him. A pounding on the door. It seemed to startle him. He grabbed my arm and pushed me into the closet, slamming the door," she said, her hand unconsciously moving up her arm to rub the bruise that was visible on her skin. "I don't know what happened next."

Jack noticed the way she nursed the area on her arm. He wasn't sure if it was just an unconscious act, or if the gesture was an indication that she was hurt. "Are you okay? Do you need to see a doctor? That bruise looks nasty."

"I'm fine," she assured him.

"Are you positive?"

"Yes."

"All right," Jack said, not wanting to pressure her.

"Let me ask you something. Did you have any contact with Richard at all when you went into the room?"

She shook her head. "No."

Jack considered her words. He knew she had just offered a plausible explanation for how the button ended up in the closet, for how the bullet casing got kicked under the bed, and for how she had gotten the bloodstains on her clothes that he had noticed earlier. And it all pointed back to Richard's killer. By Kayla's own words, the killer struggled with Richard before pulling the trigger. It was possible that's when the button came off. Panicking, the man would have turned to face Kayla standing in the doorway, and he could have kicked the bullet casing under the bed as he turned. And finally, when he grabbed Kayla and shoved her into the closet, the button could have dropped from his hand and blood from the man's own person could have transferred to her. The information she just revealed painted a vivid picture of what could have transpired. "Would you know the man if you saw him again? Would you be able to pick him out of a lineup if we needed you to?"

She looked at him helplessly. "I don't know."

"Would you be willing to try?" Jack pressed.

"Of course."

Jack nodded slightly in gratitude. "We appreciate your willingness to cooperate," he said, sitting back in the chair. He looked over at Roger Paget, the sketch artist. "Is the drawing done?" he asked the man, watching as his pencil finished shading in some areas of the paper.

Roger handed the picture to Jack so that he could look at it. "Here it is."

Jack took the picture and studied it for a moment

before showing it to Ryan. After a moment, he handed the drawing to Kayla. "I need you to look at this and let me know if this is an accurate depiction of the man you saw kill Richard tonight."

Kayla reached for the sketch with a shaky hand and looked at it closely. "It is."

Jack took the illustration back from her and handed it to a nearby officer. "Get an APB out on this guy," he said before turning back to Kayla. He tried to determine if she was up to completing the interview. The stress from his questions was taking a noticeable toll on her. He could see it in the paleness of her features, in the shakiness of her hands. "Are you okay? We just have a few more questions and then we'll be through. But if you need to take a break . . ."

Kayla immediately shook her head and took another sip from her water bottle. "I'm okay."

Jack sensed that her response was automatic. "We're almost done," he assured her.

Kayla took in a steadying breath and nodded.

Jack gave her a few moments to regroup before he continued. "We need to determine how the intruder gained access to the house, and how he left. You had mentioned that he pushed you into the closet. Did you hear any footsteps after that happened? Anything that would indicate which direction he went?"

Kayla was confused by the question. "I thought he came in through the French doors in the bedroom."

"There's no evidence to suggest that. But we did find an open window in the basement," Jack revealed.

"An open window?" she repeated, all the blood draining from her face.

Ryan looked at her in concern. "Are you okay?"

"I heard a noise early this morning, before daybreak. When I got up, Richard was already awake. He said I was hearing things."

"What kind of noise?" Jack asked.

"It was a loud thump. Richard thought I was dreaming. But if what you're saying is true, the man who shot Richard could have been in the house all day. Watching us. Waiting."

Ryan cast a quick look at Jack before turning his attention back to Kayla. "When's the last time you were in the basement?"

"Yesterday. When I was getting some things ready for the party," she said, her voice distant as she thought of the ramifications of what the detectives had said.

"Was a window left open? Did anything look out of place?" Ryan asked, trying to put together some sort of timeline.

"No."

"You sound sure of that," Jack commented.

"I'm positive. It was raining yesterday afternoon, and we have a problem with water damage in the basement. I personally locked all the windows so that no water could seep in. You can ask Ashley. She was with me."

Chapter Five

Jack's eyebrow rose slightly at the comment, but he didn't make a direct response. He would talk to Ashley later to confirm what Kayla had said. He didn't want to divert the interview. "What time were you in the basement?"

"Around one o'clock yesterday afternoon."

"And everything looked normal to you? You didn't see anything out of place?" Ryan questioned.

"No."

"Does anybody else have a key to your house?" Jack asked, running through the possible options of how someone could have entered the home.

"Only Richard's brother, Gary. But we don't see him that often."

"Why not?"

Kayla lifted a shoulder slightly in a shrug. "Richard and Gary weren't that close. There's a big gap in their ages."

"Is Gary your husband's only family?" Ryan asked.

"Yes. Richard's parents are deceased and he has no other siblings."

"When was the last time you saw Gary?"

"A couple of weeks ago. It was Richard's birthday. He turned forty-five," she replied.

Jack noticed that her attention waned after she mentioned Richard's birthday, and he quickly resumed his questioning, wanting to get her back on track. "You had mentioned that you thought you heard a thump early this morning. Did either you or Richard go into the basement to check things out?"

"I didn't. I'm not sure if Richard went down there without my knowing it," she admitted.

"You didn't ask him?" Ryan asked.

"No."

"Why not?" Jack asked.

"I guess I accepted his explanation that I was dreaming."

Jack nodded slightly and thought about the best way to broach the next segment of the interview. He needed to find out about Kayla's relationship with her husband. He couldn't ignore the absence of the man's clothes or his belongings in the bedroom. He needed to determine if there were marital problems, if there was anything going on in the relationship that would have given Kayla a reason to murder her husband. Knowing that there was no delicate way to bring up the subject, he began by warning her. "I need to talk to you about something, and it might make you a little uncomfortable."

She looked at him warily. "What?"

"When we were searching the bedroom, we didn't notice any items that might belong to Richard," Jack told her, watching her reaction as he spoke, noticing the way she tensed at the comment, the way she paled. "Were you having any problems with Richard?"

"Problems?" she repeated.

Jack's eyes narrowed slightly as he tried to determine if his question actually threw her off guard, or if she was stalling with her response. "Was there any trouble with your relationship? Anything you recently argued about?"

"I loved Richard," she assured him, her hands once more wringing the handkerchief that she held.

"Nobody's disputing that," Jack told her gently.

Kayla stared at him a moment before looking down at her hands. A full minute passed before she divulged. "Richard's been working long hours lately. He's been coming home after midnight."

"That's been going on for a while?" Jack asked, remembering Ashley's comment earlier about seeing him come home late.

"The past two months. He moved his stuff out of the bedroom just until things settled down at the office. I'm a light sleeper, and he didn't want to disturb me when he came in," she explained.

"The room he was shot in was the bedroom you use," Jack said, the words a statement, not a question.

"Yes," she confirmed. "Richard must have heard someone back there and went to investigate."

"When was the last time you talked to Richard?" Jack continued.

"About an hour before all of this happened. We were next door at the Morgans' when Richard's cell phone rang. The call had to do with business. He came inside to handle the matter."

"Do you have any idea who was on the phone?" Ryan asked.

"No. Richard didn't mention that. He just said that he had to go and take care of some things and that he would be back before the fireworks started. Shortly after that, I went to talk to Ashley. Time just sort of slipped away from there."

Jack nodded slightly, accepting her words. He knew it was entirely possible that the woman didn't have a clue regarding her husband's business dealings. A lot of people didn't share every aspect of their professional life with their spouses, himself included. "I appreciate your cooperation in talking with us."

She nodded, not responding to his comment.

"Do you have someone you could stay with tonight? You won't be able to remain here. It'll be awhile before they'll be able to release the crime scene," Jack told her gently.

"The officer called my sister before. She's on her way over here now. She was at a party out in the Hamptons, but she should be here shortly."

"Does she live on Long Island?" Jack asked.

"Yes. Not far from here."

Jack gave a brief nod of satisfaction. "We'll need you close by while the investigation progresses. I'm sure we'll have additional questions as evidence is uncovered."

"I'll help in any way I can."

"Thanks. We're going to go and check how things are going with the search. Yell if you need me, okay?" Jack instructed, rising to his feet.

"I will."

"I'll see you in a bit," he replied, waiting until Ryan

joined him before walking over to where Ed was reviewing some evidence with the uniformed officers.

Ed looked up from his task as Jack and Ryan reached him. "How did the interview go?"

Jack wearily rubbed a hand across the back of his neck. "She confirmed that it's a possibility that the window in the basement could have been opened by an intruder. She said she was down there yesterday afternoon and had locked all of the windows. But unfortunately, there's nothing concrete in any of the physical details she revealed about the man she saw shoot Richard. The description she gave is rough at best."

Ed nodded slightly in agreement. "I saw the sketch. All the guy has to do is shave his beard and remove the hat, and we have very little to go on."

"I know. And she thinks he was wearing contacts. So we can't even be sure that we know his eye color. He may have been wearing colored contact lenses," Jack said.

Ed glanced at Ryan. "What was your impression of her?"

Ryan shrugged. "It's hard to say. She seems willing to cooperate, but we've all seen other cases where the spouse was the one responsible for the murder. I don't want to rush to any judgments."

"Nobody does," Ed assured him before looking around at the activity. "It's going to be several more hours before they finish up here. They're searching the ground outside, but they're not coming up with much."

"How about the neighbors in the area? Did anyone report anything suspicious tonight?" Jack asked.

"A woman a block over claimed she heard something in her backyard, but when she turned on the light, she didn't see anything. I circulated the sketch our artist did among the reporters outside, so it should be airing about now. There's a possibility someone will call in with a tip after they see it."

"Let's hope so," Ryan said just as there was a commotion by the front door.

Jack, Ryan, and Ed glanced over at the doorway and noticed a man and woman trying to gain access to the house. The woman was arguing loudly with a uniformed officer, while the man who stood beside her tried to get her to calm down.

Ryan immediately stepped forward to find out what was going on. "Can I help you?" he asked, studying the woman who stood before him, noticing her strong resemblance to Kayla Smythe. She had the same diminutive stature, the same black hair and blue eyes, the same upturned nose and pointed chin. But where Kayla's hair was short and cut close to her head, this woman's rested below her shoulders, and was casually flipped at the ends. He recalled that Kayla had mentioned her sister was on the way over to the house, so it didn't take much for him to draw the conclusion that the woman before him was the sister Kayla would be staying with.

"I'm Lois Baker. I'd like to see my sister," she said, her tone of voice demanding.

Ryan thought that Lois Baker looked prepared to take on all comers on her sister's behalf. He was used to sizing people up, and he immediately knew that Lois Baker was a controlling force in Kayla's life. She seemed to have a strength that Kayla lacked. An edge that gave her the fortitude to go after what she wanted in life. He couldn't help but wonder if the woman's presence was going to help or hinder the investigation. "Kayla had mentioned that you were coming," he told her before shifting his gaze to the man by her side. There was something familiar about him, but Ryan couldn't put his finger on what it was. He studied him silently for a moment, trying to determine what it was about him that struck a chord. The man was tall and fit, with a full head of dark blond hair pushed ruthlessly back from his forehead, revealing brown eyes. Characteristics that Ryan had seen numerous times before on other people. There was nothing special about his features, but there was something about the man, something exclusive that made Ryan think he had seen him somewhere before. Trying to figure out where it was, he asked, "And you are?"

"Michael Baker. Kayla's brother-in-law," he responded evenly, looking past Ryan in an effort to catch a glimpse of his sister-in-law.

"Where's my sister?" Lois demanded, trying to skirt past Ryan so that she could locate her.

"She's in the living room," Ryan answered.

"Can we see her?" Michael asked, placing a supportive arm around his wife and squeezing her shoulder slightly in a gesture of comfort.

Ryan glanced briefly at Jack and Ed, and understood their unspoken message to let the couple pass. He took a step off to the side. "Of course," he said, watching as they rushed to Kayla's side.

Ryan walked back to where Jack and Ed stood. "We should question them."

"We will," Jack said, turning to watch the interaction between the Bakers and Kayla. "But right now, they're understandably upset and concerned on Kayla's behalf. It won't hurt for us to give them some time together."

Ryan followed his gaze. "They appear very close," he said, noticing how they each sat on different sides of Kayla, almost as if they were buffering her against an attack. Their concern for the woman was obvious. He couldn't miss the glances they bestowed upon her, the way that Lois Baker held her hand. Michael Baker was a little less demonstrative in his affection for Kayla, but the tenseness of his shoulders, the way he protectively sat by her side as if daring anyone to approach, was a strong indication that his loyalty rested with her.

Jack watched the animated conversation taking place between the two sisters. "The guy looks like the silent type, but Kayla's sister looks a little high-strung," he said, watching Lois. She talked as much with her hands as with her voice, and the constant movement of her arms drew attention to the large diamond she wore on her right hand.

"Mm," Ryan murmured in agreement. He stared at the man, who sat quietly while his wife did most of the talking. "It's amazing how much Michael resembles Richard, isn't it? It seems like the sisters both have the same taste in men."

"They do look a little alike. At least in build," Jack acknowledged, thinking that's where the resemblance ended. He studied Michael Baker's features. Where Richard's hair was dark in color, this man's was a dark blond. An unnatural blond. He couldn't help but think that some of the lightness of the strands came from a dye. He had seen Ashley's hair after she'd had it high-lighted, and he was almost positive that Michael Baker's was also. And though there was nothing specif-ically wrong with a man using artificial means to alter his looks, Jack couldn't help but think back to Kayla's statement that she thought the intruder had dyed his beard.

Ryan glanced at his watch, unaware of Jack's thoughts. "I think we gave them enough time to talk. Why don't we head over there and question the Bakers to see if they know anything about what might have happened here tonight."

Jack nodded and began walking across the room with Ryan.

"Mr. and Mrs. Baker?" Jack asked when they were within a few feet from where the couple sat.

Lois made brief eye contact with her husband before she acknowledged Jack. "Yes?"

Jack didn't miss the look that transpired between the two of them, and he was curious about the reason behind it. "I'm Detective Reeves, and this is Detective Parks. We'd like a moment of your time," he said, trying to get a reading on the woman.

Lois stiffened noticeably at his words and she shot an apologetic look at her sister before responding. "If this is regarding Richard's death, we have nothing to say to you right now."

Ryan's eyebrow shot up at her words. "Pardon?"

Lois Baker reached for her sister's hand and squeezed it reassuringly. "My husband and I won't say anything without our lawyer present."

Chapter Six

In the early morning hours, Jack let himself into his house. The spectators outside the Smythe residence had long since departed, and the police presence that was left was slowly dwindling. It had been a long night, and Jack was grateful that it was over. The tension that Lois Baker and her husband had brought to the atmosphere when they had arrived to collect Kayla had been tangible, and the emotional hold they had over her was obvious. Almost immediately after the couple had arrived on the scene, Kayla had withdrawn into herself. Her willingness to cooperate with the authorities had all but disappeared. With the exception of agreeing to give the forensics team her shirt so that they could determine the origin of the bloodstains on it, obtaining additional information from her had been like pulling teeth. Questions asked were answered with short, terse responses, and Jack couldn't help but wonder at the reason behind the change. It was something he would have to look into later on that day. After he got some sleep.

Locking the door with the deadbolt, he looked out the side window, noticing a patrol car pulling away from the curb. It was another signal that the search at the Smythe residence was almost complete.

"Jack?" a sleepy voice called from the couch in the living room.

Jack turned, surprised to find Ashley half-asleep on the sofa, the baby sleeping peacefully by her side. The sight caused him to smile. "Hey."

Ashley sat up and pushed a weary hand through her hair, tousling the blond tresses into disorder. "What time is it?" she asked, squinting at the clock on the wall.

"Almost four. You should be in bed."

"I wanted to wait for you."

"Hm," he murmured, walking over to the sofa and taking a seat beside her. Bending down, he placed a fleeting kiss against her lips, and slowly rubbed her back. "How are you doing?"

She reached up and brushed a lock of his gray-streaked hair off his forehead. "Me? I think the better question would be, how are you doing? The police officers that came over here for the list of people hired for the block party confirmed what Ed had told me on the phone: Richard is dead."

"Yeah."

"By the gunshot we heard," she murmured, stating the obvious.

"It looks that way."

She reached for his hand and squeezed it. "How's

Kayla holding up?" she asked, her concern for their neighbor obvious.

Jack gave a slight shrug and sighed. "As well as can be expected. She's with her sister now."

"Any ideas on who did it?"

"No. At least not yet. There was an open window in the basement, but we're not really sure if that's the way the perpetrator came into the house."

Ashley's eyes met his. "I was in the basement yesterday with her."

"I know. She told me. She said she locked all the basement windows yesterday afternoon when you two were getting things out for today's party."

"She did," Ashley confirmed. "She was concerned when she realized they were open. She made a comment about the dampness from the rain seeping into the area, and she seemed almost paranoid about locking them all."

Jack frowned at the choice of words. "Paranoid? What do you mean?"

Ashley lifted a shoulder slightly and moved to a more comfortable position on the sofa. "She seemed tense. Edgy. Almost as if she was afraid that someone would come in through one of the windows. She was also frustrated because several of the windows were sticking, and she had difficulty closing them."

"I take that to mean that she wasn't the one who opened the windows in the first place," Jack guessed.

"No. She made the comment that Richard liked to keep the windows open during the day for ventilation. She felt more secure with them closed."

"Did she ever mention if they were having a problem

with anyone?" he asked, trying to find an explanation for Kayla's apprehension. He knew that her reaction could have just been based on having a cautious nature. But for some reason, he couldn't help but think that there was more to it than that.

"No. Never."

"Do you know if something happened that frightened her? Did you question her on why she felt nervous with the windows open?"

"I asked if everything was okay."

"What was her response?"

"She just shrugged it off and said that she's been watching too many late-night movies while she waited for Richard to come home at night."

"Interesting," Jack murmured, settling back against the sofa.

"Why's that?"

"Because Richard and Kayla have been using separate bedrooms. Kayla said it was so Richard wouldn't wake her up when he came in at night. It didn't sound like she waited up for him. To the contrary, I got the impression that she was always sound asleep when he got home."

"Maybe she just made the comment to me off the cuff," Ashley suggested. "A lot of people say things that aren't meant to be taken literally."

"Possibly," Jack replied, realizing that she could be right.

"Kayla went with her sister?"

"Yeah."

"At least she has family to stay with."

"She'll need their support. She's traumatized by what occurred tonight, and there's no way that she could have stayed at the house. It'll be awhile before the crime scene's released."

"Her sister's name is Lois Baker, isn't it?"

"Have you ever met her?" Jack asked.

"No, I heard about her though."

"From Kayla?"

"Well, yes, but I also read about her in the newspaper. Her husband is being investigated for embezzlement at Kane Mortgage Corporation."

Jack stilled at her statement. "What?"

Ashley looked at him. "Her husband, Michael Baker, is being investigated for embezzlement. I'm sure you've read about it. It's been in the financial section of the paper the last several weeks."

"Wait a minute. Michael Baker. The name does ring a bell. There weren't any charges brought against him yet, if I recall," Jack said, sorting through the limited information he had read on the man. He hadn't been following the investigation closely; he hadn't even known the man was related to his neighbors. He tried to recall if Ashley had ever brought up the topic, but he couldn't think of a single instance when they had discussed it.

"No, the investigation is still going on."

"Did Kayla ever mention anything about him to you?" Jack asked.

"No. She just mentioned that her sister was going through a rough patch. She never went into any details, and I didn't think it was appropriate for me to bring it up," Ashley replied.

"You're right on that."

"You sound surprised by the news," Ashley said, watching the myriad of emotions that crossed her husband's face. "I thought I had mentioned it to you."

Jack shrugged apologetically. "If you did, I don't remember."

Ashley wasn't offended by the remark. Jack often became so engrossed in his work that his attention was diverted. She stared at him for a moment before saying, "There's something you should be aware of."

"What's that?"

"A little over a month back, Memorial Day weekend to be exact, Kayla had mentioned how upset she was that she wouldn't get to spend the weekend with her sister. Her family was renting a beach house on Fire Island, and Kayla and Richard weren't invited."

"Any idea why?"

"Kayla let it slip that her brother-in-law was having some financial problems, and her sister had come to Kayla and Richard for help. Apparently, they weren't in a position to be of assistance. There were some harsh words said, and there were a lot of hard feelings."

"So Kayla's sister blamed her for not helping?" Jack asked.

"No. Kayla's entire family held Richard totally responsible. They didn't understand why he wouldn't help out."

Jack thought back to the way Lois and Michael had rallied around Kayla that evening, lending emotional support. Though they weren't willing to talk to the police without their attorney present, there was no indication of ill will between them. If what Ashley said was true, somewhere along the way the family had mended fences. "You had mentioned that Richard and Kayla weren't in a position to help. I take it you meant financially?"

"Yes. Kayla was venting about what happened and

had mentioned that Richard had made another investment that limited their cash flow."

"Did she say what kind of investment?"

"No."

"I'll have to see what I can find out," Jack said, making a mental note to look into the matter.

"Do you think that might have something to do with
Richard's murder?" Ashley asked.

"It's possible. I won't be able to make that judgment
until I know more."

"Kayla's family should have known there would be a
good reason for Richard and Kayla not to help."

"Maybe they thought there was a different motive
behind their rejection," Jack suggested.

"Like what?"

"Spite, greed. Who knows. It could be anything.
Regardless, it's something that I'll look into later."

"If you need my help in investigating anything, let
me know."

"Maybe there is something you can do," he said,
thinking back to the information she had revealed.

"What?"

"If you could see what you can find out on Michael
Baker's case, I would appreciate it," he said, knowing
that Ashley's connections from her days as a reporter
for the newspaper would be an asset to the case.
Though Ashley had decided that she wanted to stay
home with their son during his early development
years, she still kept in touch with her colleagues. At the
moment, Jack was grateful for that. Her connections
would give him an edge in investigating Richard
Smythe's murder. Kane Mortgage wasn't a small
family-owned company. It was a fairly large corpora-

tion, and the stockholders would be following Michael Baker's embezzlement investigation very closely. It was possible that Ashley might be able to unearth something that would prove beneficial to solving Richard Smythe's murder.

"I'll call one of my friends down at the newspaper and see what they can put together for me."

"Thanks."

"It's not a problem," she assured him, suppressing a yawn.

Jack smiled. "You're tired, and so am I. Why don't we go upstairs and try and get some sleep," he suggested, rising to his feet and offering her a hand to help her up from the sofa.

"That sounds like a good idea."

After she was on her feet, Jack reached for the baby, being careful not to wake him. "I'll take John," he offered, picking up his son and holding him gently against his chest.

Ashley watched as Jack settled the baby easily into his arms. "Okay?"

"Yeah. I'll let you lead the way upstairs."

Chapter Seven

It was close to noon when Jack walked into the police station. After catching a few hours' sleep, he had spent the morning surfing the Internet, trying to find information on the embezzlement investigation of Michael Baker. But other than a few basic details, he had come up blank. Ashley had already called one of her contacts down at the newspaper to see what they had on the case. The woman she spoke to had said she would get back to her as soon as she gathered the documents. Jack hoped she got the information some time that day.

As he entered the detectives' room, he noticed that Ryan was already at his desk nursing a cup of coffee. "Hi," he greeted, heading over to the automatic coffee maker resting on a counter.

Ryan looked up at the sound of his voice. "Hi," he replied, pushing his chair back from his desk and swiveling it slightly so that he faced Jack. "I wasn't expecting you yet. I thought for sure that Ashley would need help with the baby this morning."

"Ashley's very organized in the morning. Her routine is pretty much set," Jack replied.

Ryan smiled slightly, not surprised by Jack's words. Ashley was one of the most organized people he knew. "Did you sleep okay?"

"Yeah. You?"

"Mm-hmm," Ryan murmured.

Jack took a sip from his coffee. "Is Ed in?"

"I think so. I haven't seen him yet, but I overheard some uniforms who said he was in one of the conference rooms with someone."

Jack's forehead creased in a frown. "Any idea who?"

"Not a clue. Maybe someone came in with some information about one of our pending cases."

"Maybe. But it's rare that Ed would meet with the person himself. Usually he leaves that to one of the detectives assigned to the case," Jack murmured, kicking the chair out with his foot. After taking a seat, he looked over at Ryan. "I talked to Ashley early this morning about Richard and Kayla Smythe."

"Oh?"

"She mentioned that there might be some bad blood between Richard and Kayla's family."

"That wasn't the impression I got last night."

"No, I didn't get that impression either. But apparently Michael Baker is being investigated for embezzlement. And from what Ashley had learned from Kayla, the Bakers had asked Richard for financial help at one time, and he turned them down."

Ryan leaned back in his chair at Jack's words, suddenly recalling why Michael had looked so familiar to him. He had seen his picture in the newspaper. "I knew I had seen him somewhere before. I remember reading a couple of articles on him."

"Michael Baker's investigation might explain their reluctance to talk to us last night. I tried to see if I could find out anything this morning by surfing the Web, but the details I came across were just the basics. Ashley's already been in touch with one of her contacts down at the newspaper to see what they can put together on the investigation. I'll run our own trace here so that we can compare the two. And then we need to see if we can get both Michael and Lois Baker in for questioning," Jack said, taking another sip of his coffee. "Ashley mentioned something else, though."

"What?"

"She confirmed that Kayla locked the windows in the basement the day before the murder, but she also said that according to Kayla, Richard liked the windows open."

"So Richard may have reopened the window after Kayla had closed it."

"And if Kayla was the nervous type . . ."

"Richard may not have told her," Ryan finished.

"It's something to consider," Jack murmured, glancing through the interoffice mail that was left on his desktop. Opening one of the envelopes, he scanned the documents before him. "What time did you get here this morning?"

"About a half hour before you. I would have been here sooner, but I stopped off to have breakfast with Jane this morning. Sort of a peace offering for leaving her in the lurch last night."

"That sort of thing is hard on a relationship."

"Tell me about it," Ryan grumbled.

Jack looked at Ryan with a grin while automatically reaching for another interoffice envelope and opening it. "I thought you said last night that she understood the demands of your job."

Ryan grimaced. "Apparently, I was wrong. When I got home this morning there were a couple of messages on my answering machine from her. She thought I would call her during the night to make sure she got home okay," he muttered, running a hand restlessly through his hair. "I thought I was long past the age where I had to check in with someone. I mean I knew she would get home okay. She was catching a ride with Ed's wife."

"Yeah, well, women think differently then men," Jack murmured distractedly, his attention on the document that he had in his hand.

"What do you have there?" Ryan asked, noticing Jack's preoccupation.

"The results from the gunpowder residue test from Kayla Smythe."

"And?"

"It's inconclusive."

Ryan rocked slightly in the chair. "Ed said that one of the officers stated she was sick last night. It stands to reason that she washed up after that. She wasn't tested as quickly as she should have been."

"I know."

"Did you think there was a chance that it would come back positive?" Ryan asked curiously.

"I had no idea what to think. I'm not willing to rule out Kayla's involvement in Richard's murder. We have nothing that exonerates her," Jack admitted.

"We didn't find a murder weapon at the scene last night."

"We both know that doesn't necessarily mean anything."

"True," Ryan acknowledged, falling silent while he contemplated the evidence they had uncovered at the crime scene.

"What are you thinking about?" Jack asked.

"That button you found in the closet where Kayla was."

"Yeah. That's been on my mind too."

"Do you think Kayla was the one who ripped it from Richard's shirt?"

Jack lifted a shoulder in a slight shrug. "I don't know. My first thought was that she had to have had some sort of physical contact with Richard. But that theory doesn't fall into her version of what transpired last night."

"Her distress last night seemed genuine."

"Yeah, it did. But I don't necessarily buy her explanation that the reason they had separate bedrooms was because of Richard's work hours. I think there might be more to it than that."

"Marital problems?"

"Yes."

"But you said you didn't notice any tension between the two of them," Ryan reminded him.

"I didn't, but Ashley mentioned that Kayla had watched a lot of late-night television while waiting for Richard to come home from work."

"She knows this for a fact?"

"It's what Kayla told her."

"And that contradicts Kayla's statement that the reason for the separate bedrooms was because her husband didn't want to wake her when he came in," Ryan concluded, recalling Kayla's words.

Jack shrugged. "I know that in itself doesn't necessarily mean anything, but . . ."

"But, it's not something that can be ignored. If they were having marital problems, it would give her a motive in the shooting."

"I can't argue against that. She also had the opportunity. But we still have to find the murder weapon and connect her to that for us to even begin looking at her as a serious suspect. The reality is, if Kayla is telling us the truth about what happened last night, there's a possibility that the button ended up in the closet when Richard's murderer pushed her in. She already stated that the killer struggled with Richard. Maybe the button came off then," Jack suggested.

"Maybe. But it's strange that none of Richard's stuff was in the bedroom. There wasn't even a trace left behind that he used to share the bedroom with her. To an outsider looking in, you would never know that the two of them were married from the possessions in the master bedroom."

"I think once we find the murder weapon, a lot of the pieces of the puzzle will begin to fit together. We'll be able to begin eliminating suspects."

"We should get the report from ballistics sometime today on the bullet shell we found at the crime scene."

"Let's hope so," Jack murmured just as his intercom buzzed. Reaching out, he answered the summons. "Reeves."

"Jack, I have Gary Smythe with me, Richard Smythe's brother. Meet me in the conference room in five minutes. Bring Ryan," Ed instructed.

"Sure," Jack replied, disconnecting the call. He looked at Ryan. "Richard Smythe's brother is in the conference room with Ed."

Ryan's eyebrows rose at the revelation, and he stood to his feet and reached for his suit jacket. Shrugging it on, he said, "Let's go meet the man."

Chapter Eight

Gary Smythe was sitting with Ed at the conference table when Jack and Ryan entered the room. He looked up briefly at the interruption before looking back at Ed, waiting for him to perform the introduction.

Ed stood to his feet. "Mr. Smythe, this is Detective Jack Reeves and Detective Ryan Parks. They're the lead investigators in your brother's murder investigation."

Jack immediately stepped forward to shake the man's hand. "Mr. Smythe, I'm sorry for your loss."

"Thank you. And please call me Gary."

Jack inclined his head in acknowledgment and moved over to take one of the empty seats. "I'm sorry we're meeting under these circumstances," he said, watching while Ryan shook the man's hand.

"So am I," Gary replied dejectedly, settling back in his chair. He ran an agitated hand through his short black hair, bringing attention to the recently cut strands, and also to the color of his eyes. They were brown. "I was shocked when I got the news this morning. I don't understand why Kayla didn't call me last night."

"Things were hectic at the house, and Kayla was naturally upset. I'm sure it just didn't occur to her," Jack offered by way of possible explanation.

"Maybe," Gary replied, not looking like he actually believed the explanation. "In any case, it doesn't matter now. The important thing is that we find my brother's killer. That's why I'm here, actually. I wanted to let you know that Richard has other family."

"We understand," Ryan assured him.

Gary inclined his head. "I also wanted to know if you had any ideas on who killed Richard."

Ed's gaze encompassed both Jack and Ryan. "I explained that the investigation is only just starting. Gary has offered his full cooperation to us to ensure that it progresses smoothly."

Jack glanced at Gary. "We appreciate that."

Gary shrugged off the words. "I'll answer any questions you may have. I want my brother's killer caught," he said roughly.

"We all do," Jack assured him, feeling the man's palpable tension. "Tell me, when was the last time you spoke to Richard?"

"Yesterday."

"At what time?" Jack asked.

"Shortly before noon. I called him just to check in with him. It's been a couple of weeks since I saw him."

"Kayla mentioned last night that you were at their house for Richard's birthday," Jack said.

"That's right."

"How was Richard's demeanor yesterday when you

spoke to him compared to when you saw him for his birthday?" Ryan asked.

"All right as far as I could tell. He couldn't stay on the phone long. He said he had to go and help Kayla get ready for the block party," Gary answered. He paused for a few moments before looking at Jack. "I understand you knew Richard."

"We were neighbors," Jack said, studying the man who sat before him, noticing the uncanny resemblance Gary had with his brother. Both men were of the same height and approximate weight, and their facial features were almost identical. But where Richard had been an impeccable dresser, always looking as if he was ready to close a deal, Gary seemed to be laid-back. The torn jeans that he wore and the scruffy boots made an indelible impression on Jack when he entered the room, and he noticed a heavy leather jacket resting on a coat rack. Though clean shaven, the man had an abrasive aura about him, a presence that indicated he played rough.

Gary sat back in his chair, his hands resting in his lap. "Captain Stall said you're the one who found Richard."

"Yes," Jack acknowledged.

"Was it a quick death? Did he suffer?" Gary asked bluntly, his shoulders stiff as he studied Jack.

"We didn't receive the autopsy results as of yet, but it appears to have been fairly quick, if not instantaneous."

Gary expelled a harsh breath and closed his eyes briefly at Jack's response.

"I'd like to ask you some more questions about your brother if I could," Jack told him after a moment, wanting to give him some time to compose himself.

"Of course," Gary replied.

Jack waited until he had the man's full attention before he began. "First off, do you know of anybody who had any problems with your brother? Anybody who would wish him harm?"

"Not offhand. Richard was a hard person, but I don't think he had any enemies. At least none that I'm aware of."

Ryan looked at him curiously. "Hard person? In what respect?"

Gary lifted a shoulder slightly in a shrug. "He had high ideals. He was very focused. Very driven. What Richard wanted, Richard got. He didn't always play by the rules."

"What do you mean by that?" Jack asked, realizing that the man was giving them an insight to Richard's character.

"Richard could be ruthless when he wanted to be. He went after what he wanted and he didn't care who got in the way. His eye was always on his goal," Gary said.

"That's a harsh assessment," Jack said, watching the man intently, trying to determine if he held any animosity against his brother.

"But true. I mean, don't get me wrong. I loved my brother. But I wasn't blind to his faults. He didn't get to where he is in life by cowing down to anybody," Gary said, shifting slightly in his chair and bringing his hands to the top of the table.

Jack immediately noticed an abrasion on the man's left hand. He motioned to it with his chin. "What happened?"

"What?" Gary asked.

"Your hand. That injury looks nasty," Jack said, studying the reddened, raw area that indicated the injury was recent.

Gary lifted his left hand slightly. "This? I'm afraid it was stupidity. When Kayla called me this morning to tell me what happened, I took out my frustrations on a wall."

"Did you see a doctor?" Ryan questioned, shooting a quick look at Jack. His thoughts were on the struggle that Kayla said took place between Richard and his murderer.

"No. It's not necessary. It'll heal by itself," Gary said, shrugging off the injury as of little importance.

Jack studied Gary Smythe. Though his words indicated that he could care less about his injury, Jack couldn't help but notice that he immediately removed his injured hand from the table. It was a sign that the man wasn't comfortable with the questions. Not wanting to put him on the defensive, Jack brought the conversation back to the man's brother's death. "You had mentioned that Kayla called you."

"Yes."

"About what time was that?" Jack asked, trying to put together a timeline. He wanted to find out where Gary Smythe was last night without raising the man's suspicions. The injury that he sported automatically put him under suspicion for his brother's death. And the characterization he gave of Richard indicated that he had firsthand knowledge of what Richard was willing to do to get what he wanted in life. He couldn't help but wonder if Richard had done something to his brother that would have given him a motive for his death.

"About four–thirty this morning. She said she was with her sister, Lois," Gary answered.

"What were you doing when she called?" Jack continued.

"Sleeping. I had gotten home a couple of hours earlier."

Jack leaned back in his chair, hearing it creak under his weight. "You were out? Can I ask where?"

"I was at a friend's house. Jimmy Cooper. He had a party for the Fourth," Gary replied.

"Were there a lot of people present?" Ryan asked.

"A fair amount. I ride a Harley. The people at the party were the ones that I normally ride with."

"Did the people at the party know your brother?" Ryan asked.

"They've met. I can't say how well they knew him. Richard was a little more conservative than they are. I doubt if they would have found a lot in common with each other."

"We'd like to get a list of the attendees with their phone numbers and addresses if at all possible," Ryan said.

Gary looked over at Ryan, a frown marring his features. "Do you think one of them had something to do with Richard's death?"

"Right now, we just need to cover all the bases. Is giving us the list going to be a problem?" Ryan asked.

After a long pause of silence, Gary responded. "No."

Jack didn't miss his hesitation. "It's procedure," he assured him.

Gary nodded. "I understand."

Jack held the man's gaze for a moment. "You had mentioned that your friends met Richard before. When was that?"

"At my daughter's christening party," Gary said, his facial expression softening.

"How many children do you have?" Jack asked.

"Just one," Gary replied, reaching into his pocket for his wallet. Opening it up, he showed them a snapshot of his daughter with Richard and Kayla at the christening. "My brother was her godfather."

Jack glanced at the photo. "Your daughter's beautiful."

"Thanks. She looks like my wife," Gary replied, showing the photo briefly to both Ryan and Ed before putting his wallet away. "Richard was so proud that day. He always wanted children, so I think my daughter had a special place in his heart."

Ryan looked over at him at his words. "Richard and Kayla didn't have any children, did they?"

"No."

"I guess it's hard to start a family when you're focusing on your career," Ryan acknowledged.

"Yeah, but that wouldn't have stopped Richard. He's always had a soft spot for kids. He practically raised me when we were growing up. My father died when I was young, and my mother worked two jobs."

"That must have been tough," Jack sympathized, hoping the man would continue to speak on his own accord.

"It was. I think that's part of what motivated Richard. He saw how hard my mother had to work for practically nothing. He swore that he would never be in the position of living paycheck to paycheck."

"So he dedicated himself to his career," Jack said, understanding Richard's drive to succeed.

"Yeah. He put himself through college at night and worked full time during the day, trying to get ahead. After he made it, he wanted me to go to college. He offered to finance it. He didn't want my family to struggle the way we did growing up," Gary replied.

"Did you take him up on his offer?" Ryan asked.

"No. School was never my thing. I can honestly say that was a point of contention in our relationship. Richard didn't understand that we had different interests in life," Gary murmured, his thoughts on his brother.

"It sounds as if your brother cared about you," Ryan said.

"That I never doubted."

"What did Kayla think about your relationship with your brother?" Jack asked.

Gary expelled a small breath. "Kayla and I never quite saw eye-to-eye. I don't think she approves of my lifestyle. Even though she doesn't work, she shares the same ambition as Richard. Her family believes that the man in the family should be the breadwinner. And even though I make a decent living as a mechanic, I don't think it lives up to her standards."

"You're a mechanic?" Ryan asked.

"I own my own shop."

"And Kayla has an issue with that?"

"As I said, she has standards."

"It sounds like it's her problem," Ryan said.

Gary shrugged. "I agree. Unfortunately, she caused some problems for my brother and me. We never spent the holidays together because Richard and Kayla were always with her family."

"That must have caused some resentment on your part."

"I had my own family at home to worry about. I really couldn't concern myself too much with Kayla's. Richard was a grown man, more than capable of making his own decisions. I'm sure he had his own reasons for whatever he did."

"Did Richard ever say anything to you about Kayla's family?" Jack asked.

"Like what?"

"What his feelings were toward them?"

Gary thought seriously about the question before answering. "Things weren't always smooth if you know what I mean."

Jack leaned forward in his chair, his elbows resting on the table. "Could you be more specific? Was anything ever said in front of you by anyone in the family or by Richard?"

"There were a couple of times when everybody was together where some sparks flew. Kayla's family isn't shy about expressing their opinions. If they didn't like something that Richard and Kayla were doing, they were quick to point out to them what they should be doing."

"Can you think of any specific incidences?" Ryan questioned.

"The one where Kayla wanted to remodel the kitchen comes to mind. She and Richard had everything all picked out until her sister told her that she should go a different route. By the end of the night, the order for the cabinets had been canceled. I know that doesn't sound like much, but it did cause some trouble between Richard and Kayla."

"So you would say Kayla's family was controlling," Jack concluded, thinking back to Lois Baker's attitude back at the house, how almost instantly upon the Bakers arrival, Kayla had clammed up. Gary only confirmed what they already knew.

Gary laughed, but it was without humor. "That description is mild. Kayla's sister would do just about anything to get what she wanted. She was a lot like Richard in that respect. I don't know if you're aware of this or not, but Lois and her husband are having financial problems. They were at Richard and Kayla's house the night of his birthday, and they were very vocal about his unwillingness to help them out of a tight situation."

Jack's eyes narrowed slightly. "What do you mean by that?"

"They laid a guilt trip on Kayla. Lois Baker told her that if Richard didn't help them out, he would regret it."

Chapter Nine

Thirty minutes later, Jack, Ryan, and Ed were alone in the room. Gary Smythe had just left with the promise of getting them the list of people who were at the barbecue he attended the previous day.

"So what did you think?" Ed asked, leaning back in his chair and tapping his pen against the table. He had been comfortable letting Jack and Ryan take the lead in questioning Gary Smythe. He had already interviewed the man, and sitting quietly while Jack and Ryan spoke gave him the opportunity to observe Gary Smythe's responses, his mannerisms.

"I think we need to look closely at Gary Smythe. His hair was recently cut, his face cleanly shaven, and he has a fresh abrasion on his hand. All three things are possibilities in what we're looking for in our shooter. And he also has brown eyes—a trait Kayla was sure that Richard's killer possessed," Jack said.

"You think Gary is the person Kayla saw kill

Richard?" Ryan asked, thinking about the description they got from her last night, the sketch their artist made.

"It's not something we can rule out."

Ed thought about Jack's words. "Wouldn't Kayla have recognized her own brother-in-law?"

Jack lifted a shoulder in a slight shrug. "Maybe not. If everything happened as quickly as she said it did when she walked into the bedroom, I don't know if she would have been focused entirely on the killer. She would have had only a fleeting glimpse of the guy. It's possible that she caught certain characteristics of the killer's face, and her mind filled in the blanks."

Ryan considered Jack's response before glancing at Ed. "Jack's right. There's a lot about Gary Smythe that we need to know more about. By the man's own admission, his brother was a hard man, and I didn't get the impression he was enthralled with Kayla."

"I was watching his reactions closely while you two were questioning him. Even though he agreed to give us his fingerprints, I saw the way he took his injured hand out of sight when you mentioned it," Ed said.

Jack looked at Ed. "Did you notice the injury when you met him this morning?"

"I did. But I also knew I was going to bring the two of you in to meet with him. I didn't want to say anything about it before you two got here, in case it made him nervous."

"That was probably a smart move," Ryan said.

Ed looked down at the notes he took during the interview. "It's possible that his friends might be able to fill in some blanks about the guy's true relationship with Richard."

Jack glanced at his watch. "He said he'll get the list to us sometime this afternoon. If it's not too late, Ryan and I will start doing the rounds. Depending on how many people are listed, we might be able to make a dent in the interview process."

"Sounds good," Ed replied, leaning back in his chair and folding his hands across his chest. "Maybe after tonight, we'll have a better understanding of Gary Smythe and any possible tie he may have to his brother's murder."

Jack nodded and stretched his legs out under the table, making himself more comfortable. "What's the status on the background checks we requested last night? Have you received anything?"

"Not yet. We should start getting preliminary reports sometime this afternoon, and I'll get the ball rolling on the other background checks we'll need on the list from Gary as soon as he gives it to us. If his friends are anything like him, it'll make for some interesting reading if nothing else," Ed said.

Ryan was quiet for a moment before asking, "Anything show on the evidence collected last night?"

Ed shook his head slightly. "No, but it's early yet. I would say we should start getting results sometime late today, early tomorrow."

"I already got Kayla's gunpowder residue test," Jack said.

"And?" Ed prompted.

"It's inconclusive."

"That's not surprising. The search team is heading back to Richard and Kayla's house today to do a final run-through before we release the crime scene. Maybe they'll pick up more clues. Though to be honest, I'm not expecting it. Everyone was pretty thorough yesterday," Ed said.

"We'll have to see what we can come up with on Kayla's family, especially her sister and brother-in-law. It sounds like they may have had a motive to want the man out of the picture," Ryan suggested.

"If Lois is as controlling as she seems, it's possible she'll see Richard's death as an opportunity to take control of Kayla's assets," Jack said.

"How soon do you guys want to bring her in for questioning?" Ed asked.

"Today works for me," Jack replied. "I'll call and see if I can arrange it for later this afternoon. She was adamant last night about her and her husband not speaking to us without their attorney present, so I'm pretty sure she was on the phone with him first thing this morning. Us bringing them in should be no surprise."

Ryan glanced at Jack and Ed. "That'll give us some time to pull the details on the investigation going on about her husband."

"Embezzlement, isn't it?" Ed asked.

"Yeah," Jack acknowledged.

"I think I read something about it in the papers. I didn't make the connection until I spoke to Gary Smythe. The investigation might explain the man's reticence to talk to us last night," Ed said.

Jack laughed, but it was without humor. "Reticence? The guy barely spoke a word last night."

"Yeah, well, knowing about the problems he's having goes a long way to explain that," Ed replied.

"Possibly," Jack said, knowing he wanted an explanation from the man himself. "I'll try and get her husband to accompany her today, so we can interview both of them." He paused for a moment before continuing. "By the way, what time did you get here this morning?" he asked Ed.

"I got the call from the desk sergeant about ten. I was here by ten thirty."

"Gary Smythe wasted no time in coming down," Ryan said.

"No, he didn't," Ed agreed.

"What was your first impression of him?" Jack asked curiously.

"Honestly? He reminded me of a man who has no problem taking the law into his own hands."

"He has a tough aura about him," Ryan agreed.

"Yeah, he does. And based on my impression, I think it's possible that if he had a problem with Richard, he would have confronted him," Ed said.

"That doesn't necessarily mean he would have killed him," Ryan pointed out.

"No, you're right," Jack agreed. "But it's possible that Richard's death was unintentional."

"Meaning?" Ed prompted.

"Maybe Gary went to see Richard to talk about something. They could have argued. It's possible things just got out of control."

"Kayla did say that she saw the person who shot Richard arguing with him first," Ryan recalled.

"It'll be easy enough to check if Gary has any guns registered in his name," Ed said, standing to his feet. "Why don't we head back to our area and see if anything else came in on this case. We can finish this discussion there."

Chapter Ten

An hour later, Jack was at his desk finishing a telephone call with Lois Baker. Hanging up the receiver, he swiveled slightly in his chair, a pensive expression on his face.

"What did she say?" Ryan asked, hearing only one side of the conversation. He had sat quietly while Jack made the call, but he couldn't help but detect the tension in Jack's voice as he spoke to Lois.

Jack turned his chair to look at Ryan. "She said today's not a good day for her to come down to the station. Apparently, her attorney's in court. She promised she would be here tomorrow at ten."

"With her husband?"

"So she says."

"We could always force the issue today and bring them in anyway," Ryan suggested, knowing that the idea wasn't in the investigation's best interest. It would only put the Bakers on the defensive, more so than they currently were. Ideally, they needed their cooperation. They wanted them relaxed enough where they might say something that would give them a handle on the case. And though they could take action and bring the couple in, nobody could make them talk if they weren't willing.

Jack's thoughts followed the same pattern as Ryan's. "I really don't want to take that avenue if we can avoid it. If they don't talk, we wouldn't be able to hold them long without pressing charges. And that's not something we're in a position to do. We have no evidence that ties either of them to Richard's murder."

"It's an option. You have to admit that their behavior is odd considering what happened."

"Yeah, I know. But the reality is, we're not even twenty-four hours into the investigation. Waiting until tomorrow morning to talk to them won't hurt our case. They're not going anywhere. Kayla's staying with them. They're not a flight risk."

Ryan lifted a shoulder in a slight shrug. "I'll go along with however you want to handle this."

"Then let's give it until tomorrow morning. If they stall, then we'll force the issue," Jack said.

Ryan looked at Jack curiously. "Did you get the impression that's what Lois was doing? Stalling?"

"A little,' Jack admitted. "She's definitely reluctant to talk to us. That much is obvious."

"Do you think she's covering up something?"

"Possibly. It could just be that she's nervous about her husband's current legal problems."

"Maybe," Ryan agreed.

"Did you get the chance to look at the information that came in on Michael Baker?" Jack asked, motioning to the report that had been completed by the police department personnel.

"Yeah. It made for interesting reading."

"But not earth-shattering."

"No, you're right there. Other than statistical information, we don't have too much to work with," Ryan said just as he heard the sound of footsteps. He glanced toward the doorway before looking at Jack. "You have company."

Jack frowned and quickly swiveled his chair to see what Ryan was talking about. A smile came over his face when he saw Ashley walking toward him. He stood and walked over to meet her. "Hey," he said, bending down to kiss her cheek. "Where's John?"

"With Mrs. Foley," Ashley replied with a wry smile, referring to another one of their neighbors. "I mentioned to her that I needed to see you, and she said I'd be doing her a favor if I let her watch him for a few hours. I think she was appalled at the idea of him coming to a police station."

Jack laughed. "She is a little strait-laced," he agreed, thinking about their prim and proper neighbor.

"Maybe in this instance, she's right. This really isn't a place for a baby," Ashley murmured, looking through the open doorway to where a man in handcuffs was arguing with his arresting officer.

Jack followed her gaze and grimaced at the sobering image. "No, it's not," he agreed.

"John's safe with her."

"I know. She's one of the most responsible people I know. We'll have to get her something as a token of our appreciation."

"I'll stop at the nursery on the way home and pick

her up a plant," Ashley promised, thinking of the lady's fondness for plants and flowers.

"Sounds good," Jack said, turning to walk back to his desk. He held out a chair for Ashley before resuming his own seat. "So tell me, what brings you down here?"

Ashley didn't answer Jack right away. Instead she looked over at Ryan and smiled. "Hi, Ryan."

"Hi, Ashley," Ryan replied.

"How's Jane?"

"Good, thanks."

"I was sorry you couldn't join us for the barbecue yesterday."

Ryan shrugged apologetically. "We were too. But Jane had already promised her parents that we would go to their place."

"I understand."

"Ashley . . ." Jack prompted when it didn't look like she was going to explain the reason for her visit.

Ashley turned her attention back to her husband. "You're so impatient," she murmured teasingly, reaching for her tote bag. She removed a file and handed it to him. "I have the information from the newspaper on Michael Baker."

Jack took the manila file. "That was quick."

"It pays to have connections."

"That it does," Jack said, opening the file to read the contents.

Ryan rolled his chair over to Jack's desk. "What does it say?" he asked, glancing over at the report.

"The investigation on Michael Baker has been going on for well over a year," Jack murmured, reading through the document.

"A year?" Ryan asked.

"That's what the reporter's notes say," Jack said, not looking up from his task.

"That's a long time. I read through the briefing we were able to pull from our own sources. That said the Feds have only been investigating the guy for six months," Ryan said.

"The notation in this file is quoting a source at Kane Mortgage Company. It could be that the company did it's own internal investigation before getting the FBI involved," Jack replied.

Ryan looked over at Ashley. "How close are you to Kayla?"

"If you're asking me if she ever mentioned any of this to me, I'm afraid not," she responded.

Ryan's brow creased in a frown, and he turned his attention back to Jack. "What else does the file say?"

"There's some detailed comments about what caused the suspicion to focus on Michael Baker. Apparently, when the money started disappearing, Michael Baker's lifestyle took a turn for the better. He started showing up in custom tailored suits, and began driving a new car. From what this report says, his co-workers in the office noticed a big change in both his appearance and his lifestyle. Expensive lunches, long weekend trips, things of that nature," Jack revealed.

"So they drew their own conclusions on what was going on," Ryan murmured, sitting back in his chair and tilting it on its axle.

"Yep. There was no explanation to account for his sudden windfall. Apparently, the company had both a hiring and raise freeze in place. His co-workers already knew that the money shouldn't have been coming from

Michael's salary, and they also knew that Lois didn't work," Jack said.

"Did they find the money trail?" Ryan asked.

"No. There's nothing in here to indicate that," Jack said, reading the rest of the file before handing it to Ryan.

"The case is circumstantial," Ashley pointed out. "There's enough to get an indictment, hence the investigation, but I'm not sure it'll be enough to put Michael in prison."

"But it is enough to have totally ruined his reputation," Jack said.

"That's a fact," Ryan agreed, closing the file and placing it on his desk. "If Michael went to Richard Smythe for help to extradite him from this mess, and Richard refused . . ." he said, letting the rest of the sentence go unsaid.

"It might have been enough to put him over the edge," Jack finished just as his phone rang. He answered the summons. "Reeves."

There was a long pause of silence as the caller spoke to Jack, and Ashley and Ryan looked at him expectantly as he hung up the phone.

"That was Kayla. She asked if I would meet with her at the diner on Main Street," Jack said.

Ryan glanced at his watch. "What time?"

"She's there now."

"Then let's go," Ryan said, getting to his feet and reaching for his suit jacket.

Jack held up a hand to stop him. "She asked to meet with me alone."

Ryan sat back down. "Alone?"

"That's what the woman said."

"Any idea why?" Ashley asked, looking at Jack.

"She doesn't want to draw attention to herself. At least that's what she told me."

"She's frightened of something," Ryan concluded.

"She's giving that impression," Jack agreed, getting to his feet and reaching for his suit jacket. He shrugged into the garment.

"Are you sure that you don't want me to come? I can wait in the car," Ryan told him.

"No. I don't want her to feel like she can't trust me. I'll see you later," Jack told Ryan while reaching for Ashley's hand. "Come on. I'll walk you to your car."

"Call me and let me know what's going on," Ryan called after him.

Jack raised a hand in acknowledgment, but didn't turn to look his way. "You got it."

Chapter Eleven

The diner on Main Street was only half full when Jack arrived. Most of the lunch crowd had already departed, and only a few tables were occupied as the waitresses scrambled around getting the tables ready for dinner. As he stepped into the air-conditioned restaurant, he paused for a moment, letting his eyes adjust to the dim light. Reaching up, he removed his sunglasses and looked around, searching the sea of faces for Kayla's.

He spotted her sitting alone at a corner table, and was somewhat surprised by her appearance. It was almost as if she was trying to disguise herself. Her hair was all but covered by a colorful silk scarf, and fashionable sunglasses shielded her eyes from curious onlookers. Her denim jeans and shirt were baggy, reflecting nothing of the designer clothes that she normally favored. Her whole appearance baffled him. If he hadn't known that she would be there, if he hadn't been looking for her, he never would have recognized her.

When she looked up and caught his eye, he offered her a small smile and slowly made his way over to where she sat. "Kayla," he greeted as he came within touching distance of her table.

She didn't return his smile. Instead she reached out to grasp his hand, the urgency of her grip reflecting her inner emotional turmoil. "Jack. Thank you for coming."

He squeezed her hand slightly and slid into the booth. "You sounded upset on the phone."

"I just didn't know who else to turn to," she said, reaching up to remove her sunglasses, revealing eyes that shimmered with tears. She dabbed at her eyes with a handkerchief she clutched in her hand.

Jack's forehead creased with concern when he saw her emotional state. "Did something else happen?"

"No, things are just so out of control right now. I needed to talk to someone familiar. I hope you don't mind that I called you."

"Of course not," he assured her, ordering a cup of coffee from the waitress when she stopped by the table. He noticed the woman looking at him and Kayla curiously before she left to get his order, and he looked at Kayla sympathetically. "She's just concerned that you're so upset."

"I guess meeting here wasn't the best idea," Kayla murmured, sliding her sunglasses back onto her face.

"It's as good a place as any," Jack said, glancing once more around at the nearly empty restaurant. The tables close to theirs were empty, and the other diners looked engrossed in their own conversations. He wasn't really concerned that they would be overheard.

Kayla expelled a small breath that caught on a sigh. "I wanted to talk to you about last night."

"Did you remember something that you didn't mention?"

"No. I wanted to apologize for my sister's behavior. I know Lois came on as a little overbearing, and I wanted to assure you that she's not normally like that. I also didn't want you to think that I would allow her to keep me from talking with you. I loved my husband a great deal, and I'll do anything you need me to do to find his killer," she said, fidgeting slightly with the handkerchief that she held.

"I didn't think that you wouldn't help with Richard's murder investigation. And as to your sister's behavior, you don't owe me any apologies," Jack assured her, knowing that he couldn't hold her responsible for her sister's actions.

"Thank you for that, but Lois acted inappropriately last night. I know that, you know that, and I think Lois is honest enough to admit to it. Even Michael made a comment to her when we left my house," she said, falling silent when the waitress arrived with his coffee.

Jack waited until the waitress left before responding. "What exactly did Michael say?"

"Just that he didn't think it was necessary for them to have their attorney present before they spoke with you. He told her that there shouldn't have been any hesitation on their part to help the police with Richard's murder investigation."

Jack recalled the man's behavior the night before. He had barely said a word, and gave no indication that he wasn't willing to go along with his wife's insistence that their attorney be present for the questioning. "Why didn't he say anything to Lois when we tried to question them?"

"I'm not sure. Maybe he didn't want to embarrass her."

"Did Lois or Michael ask you to meet with me?" he asked bluntly, curious if this meeting was supposed to be some sort of smoke screen to protect her sister, to protect her brother-in-law. His first thought upon seeing Kayla at the diner was that she was upset over what had happened to Richard. That she wanted to tell him something that might help with the investigation. That someone may have contacted her, and she might have a clue about who murdered him. But now, he wasn't so sure. She seemed to be making excuses for her sister and brother-in-law, as if trying to smooth over any indiscretions the couple may have made. Jack couldn't get a handle on whether Kayla was doing it on her own, or if she was asked to intercede on their behalf. He knew it was possible that Kayla was trying to create a buffer for their interview tomorrow with the police. Her family appeared to have a strong hold over her, and the way she just came to their defense only reinforced that.

"No."

She answered a little too quickly for Jack to believe her, but he didn't call her on it. Instead he reached for the creamer and poured a small amount into his cup before stirring the beverage. "Does Lois know you're here?" he asked.

"No. To be honest, she would be upset if she found out."

That Jack could believe. But instead of saying what

was on his mind, he decided to see if he could get her to open up. Now that he knew that nobody had openly threatened her, he wanted to use this meeting to his advantage. It didn't matter to him why she felt the need to meet with him privately, he figured that he would find out in time. The important thing at the moment was that he had the opportunity to talk to her one-on-one, with no interference. He relaxed in the booth, his body language inviting her to do the same. Taking a sip of his coffee, he asked, "Why's that?"

She shrugged and grasped her coffee cup in both hands, as if taking comfort from its warmth. There was a long stretch of silence before she answered. "I don't know. She's been different since the investigation began on Michael," she said, watching him as she said the words.

"Are you asking me in a roundabout way if I know anything about what's going on with your brother-in-law?"

"Do you?" she countered.

Jack took another sip from his coffee before answering. "I know what's been in the newspapers."

She grimaced. "You can't believe everything you read. Or believe everything you hear."

Jack sensed that she was trying to tell him something by her cryptic comments. "I realize that. I'll make up my own mind after I talk to the man."

His words seemed to calm whatever fear she had. "I'm sorry. I don't mean to be so mysterious. It's just that I know Ashley still has a lot of contacts at the newspaper, and the reporters covering the story haven't always been kind to Michael."

"Kindness doesn't sell newspapers."

"No, I know. But I wanted you to know that there's more to Michael than what's been reported."

Her words gave him pause. It occurred to Jack that he may have stumbled across the reason for her wanting to speak with him. She was concerned about what Ashley might find out from her contacts at the newspaper. She was literally trying to find out what the police had uncovered. "I wouldn't worry too much about what the newspapers say," he told her, avoiding touching on the topic of what actually was revealed in the reports they had obtained. "The police aren't going to jump to conclusions. We're used to dealing with biased reporting."

She relaxed slightly at his words. "I overheard Lois talking to you on the phone earlier."

"Did you?"

"Yes. I understand that she's meeting with you tomorrow?"

"Tomorrow morning. Michael will be joining her," he told her, not seeing any harm in her knowing.

"I'd like you to keep an open mind when you talk to them. My sister especially. Lois has a strong personality, but she's always been very good to me. I don't want you to get the wrong impression from speaking with her."

"If she's honest with me, that won't happen."

She watched him quietly for a moment before nodding. "I just don't want my sister to become a scapegoat in Richard's death."

"She won't. But that doesn't mean I'm not interested in talking to her. Or her husband for that matter. I think they can both prove beneficial to the investigation," Jack said.

"Lois and Michael will help in any way they can," she assured him.

"That's all I ask."

"Thank you."

"Feel better?"

"Yes, thanks," she said, looking at him apologetically. "I'm sorry if I seem a little neurotic when it comes to my sister and her family. It's just with everything going on, I don't think Lois could handle any more pressure."

Jack didn't respond to her statement. "Do you mind if I ask you some questions?"

"Of course not."

"How exactly did your husband and sister get along?"

"All right, I guess. They weren't exactly crazy about each other, but they tolerated each other for my sake."

Jack's eyes narrowed slightly. "Any animosity there?"

"No."

"How about Michael? How did he get along with Richard?"

"Good. They were golf buddies. They met at a course out east at least once a week for a game."

"So they were friendly," Jack deduced from her words.

"I would say so."

"My next question might seem a little personal, but I really need to know the answer," he said, watching her as she mentally braced herself for the words. "Did Lois and Michael ever come to you for money?"

She hesitated only briefly before answering. "Yes, but it's not what you're thinking."

"Right now, I'm not thinking anything. I'm only trying to find answers to make sense of this all."

"I understand."

"Then help me."

Kayla's eyes met his while she tried to determine if she could trust him. Finding the answer in his gaze, she began speaking. "Lois and Richard were having some cash flow problems about a year ago. It wasn't that they didn't have money, it was just that it was all tied up in investments."

"Couldn't they have cashed in some stock?"

"Actually, that's what they ended up doing. Even though Michael knew they were going to take a loss, he knew there was no other alternative. Richard arranged for him to do it at his brokerage firm."

"So the influx of money that Michael's company became suspicious of was actually his own," Jack murmured, getting a clear picture of where this was going.

"Yes. It's unfortunate that the money started disappearing from Michael's company at the same time. People started to talk, and the gossip took over. It wasn't long before Michael started hearing the tales."

"He didn't set the record straight?"

"No. He wouldn't. That's not his nature. He's actually a pretty private person. He just ignored the talk, hoping that it would eventually die down. He had no idea of the internal investigation that was going on. Anyway, auditors were called in. They found a paper trail that led to an offshore account in the name of Caldwell."

"So?"

"Caldwell is Michael's mother's maiden name. It's also his middle name," Kayla said.

Jack frowned. "You think someone set him up?"

"I do," she replied earnestly. "I think whoever it was watched Michael closely. The account that they found was opened about the same time Michael sold his stock."

"Does Michael have any idea who's behind it?"

"Not a clue. When the investigation turned in his direction, whatever money he and Lois had left in assets was allocated for his legal counsel. Lawyers don't come cheap. It wasn't until they ran through their own money that they came to Richard and myself for help."

"When was that?" Jack asked, remembering his conversation with Ashley that it was sometime around Memorial Day. He was curious if Kayla would confirm what Ashley said.

"In May. Unfortunately, Richard and I weren't in a position to help out. And I have to be honest, it caused some hard feelings within my family."

"But the hard feelings didn't last."

"No. Blood is thick. Most families go through some tough patches. It doesn't mean that you write the person off for good. After I explained everything to Lois and Michael, things sorted themselves out."

"Do you mind if I ask why you couldn't help out?" Jack asked, fully realizing the personal nature of the question. He wasn't sure if she would respond, but he had to try to get as much information as possible.

When she didn't immediately reply, he prompted, "Kayla?"

She took a deep breath before saying, "We didn't have the money to give them. Richard had lent his brother, Gary, money for a home."

Chapter Twelve

An hour later, Jack made his way back into the police station. Walking into the detectives' room, he saw Ryan studying a document. "What do you have there?" he asked by way of greeting.

Ryan glanced up at the sound of his voice. "Hey. I wasn't sure what time to expect you back. You didn't call."

Jack lifted a shoulder in a slight shrug. "There was no reason to. There wasn't any information Kayla gave me that I needed you to look into before I got back." He motioned to the paper that Ryan held in his hands. "You never answered my question. What are you looking at?"

Ryan held up the document before placing it on his desk. "This? It's just the list that Gary Smythe promised us."

Jack walked over to the coffeemaker to pour himself a cup of the strong brew. "How many people are listed?"

"About ten. I thought if you're up to it, we could head out this afternoon and start interviewing them. There's a note that a few of them hang out at a pool hall. We can swing by and at least see if they're available to talk to."

"Sounds okay by me."

"Then as soon as you finish your coffee, we'll get started. But in the meantime, you can tell me exactly what Kayla wanted to see you about."

Jack carried his coffee back to his desk and took a seat. "Nothing specific. I got the impression she found out about our meeting with her sister and brother-in-law tomorrow. I think she was just trying to do some damage control after her sister's behavior yesterday. She also seemed concerned about what we might dig up on Michael Baker."

"Concerned as if she was trying to cover up something?" Ryan asked, looking for an explanation for her behavior.

"I'm not sure. She appears to have a strong sense of loyalty to her family. It could just be protective instincts making their way to the forefront."

"And the purpose of her meeting with you alone? Any idea on the reason behind that?"

"The lady's nervous. There's no doubt about it. She's definitely afraid of drawing attention to herself right now."

Ryan considered Jack's words. "I guess that's understandable. When you met with her this afternoon, did she say anything that might be relevant to the investigation?"

Jack took a sip of his coffee before answering. "Possibly. She told me about the Bakers' money problems. She mentioned that she and Richard weren't in a position to help them financially."

"Did she offer an explanation on the reason?"

Jack inclined his head. "It's because they lent the money to Gary Smythe so that he could buy a house."

Ryan sat back in his chair and expelled a small breath. "Something Gary failed to mention. That casts more suspicion on him."

"I agree. And maybe after we get done interviewing his friends, we'll have a much better handle on the guy."

Ryan nodded and motioned to the folders on his desk. "Some of our reports came in while you were gone."

"Which ones?"

"The background reports, ballistics, the preliminary autopsy report, and the report of the bloodstains on Kayla's shirt."

"And?" Jack prompted.

Ryan reached for several folders and pushed them across the desk in Jack's direction. "Take a look."

Jack reached for the files and opened the one pertaining to the background checks. "It doesn't look like we uncovered much," he said as he read through the reports on Kayla, Gary, Lois, and Michael. "All of this stuff we were able to find out on our own. There's no history of violence, traffic violations, or crimes for any of them, with the exception of the investigation going on with Michael," he said, scanning through all the data before placing the folder back on the desk. He tapped the cover of the manila folder with his fingers. "There's nothing here that's going to get us any closer to finding out who murdered Richard."

"No, you're right. That information doesn't. But the report on Richard is a different story. It's in a separate file. Take a look."

Jack glanced at Ryan curiously while he shifted the folders for the one on Richard. Opening the cover, he skimmed through the documents, noticing several police reports for traffic violations. "The guy was a careless driver."

"Yeah, he was. But if you keep looking, you'll find a report on the accident Kayla had mentioned to us."

Jack sorted through the papers until he found the report in question. "What am I looking for?" he asking, not seeing anything that should raise any red flags.

"Look at the name of the other party involved."

"Carl Taylor. What about it?"

Ryan pushed the list Gary had given him across the desk in Jack's direction. "He's an acquaintance of Gary Smythe's."

Jack's forehead puckered in a frown as he looked at the list and compared the information to their report. "Same address."

"Yeah. And if you notice, there's a note that he hangs out in the pool hall we'll be visiting this afternoon."

"Kayla never mentioned that the person who had the confrontation with Richard was a friend of Gary's."

"Maybe she didn't know. From what Gary told us, he and Kayla didn't have that close of a relationship. It's possible she was completely in the dark about it," Ryan suggested.

"So the question is, just how often did Richard see the man, and were there any other problems that we should be aware of?"

Ryan motioned with his chin to the file. "Based on everything in there, it could be that we're dealing with a case of road rage. The guy accused Richard of cutting him off deliberately."

"You think that's a possible motive for Richard's death?"

"Maybe."

"It's plausible," Jack said, considering the information before him. He knew that the idea wasn't totally out of the realm of possibilities.

"It's something we need to check out."

Jack nodded and drained the remainder of his coffee before opening the other folders to read through the autopsy report and the ballistics information. "The bullet casing we found at the scene of the crime matched the bullet removed from Richard."

"Which means only one shot was fired."

"It was fired at close range. One shot was all it took. Unfortunately, there's no way to determine if our killer was an expert marksman, or a first-time gun user."

"If you look at the autopsy report, there are no marks or bruises on Richard's body other than the gunshot wound. Kayla mentioned that Richard struggled with the intruder. There's nothing to indicate that happened."

"Maybe they just struggled with the gun."

"Possibly. Without the actual murder weapon, we'll never know."

"The only blood they were able to find on Kayla's shirt matched Richard's," Jack said.

"The amount was minimal."

Jack expelled a small sigh and placed the files back on the desk. "We need a lot more information before we'll have any answers. Why don't we head out and see what we find."

Thirty minutes later, Jack and Ryan arrived at Mo's, a local pool hall in the area that catered to bikers. The parking lot was full of motorcycles, and several men wearing black leather jackets were standing outside with their bikes, smoking.

"It seems like an interesting place," Ryan said.

"That it does," Jack murmured as he parked the unmarked police car. Though there were a few cars present, the majority of the vehicles were motorcycles. "It looks like a tough crowd," he said as he noticed some bikers leaning against the outside brick wall. Most were dressed in torn jeans and T-shirts, and the tattoos they sported were visible from Jack's vantage point.

"We've both dealt with worse," Ryan said, reaching into his pocket for the small notebook he carried that contained the names of the list of people that Gary Smythe had given them. Glancing at it, he familiarized himself once more with the names. "According to Gary's notes, at least five of the people hang out here. The rest we'll have to track down at their homes. It shouldn't be that difficult. They all live in the same neighborhood."

"Yeah, I noticed that too," Jack told him while reaching for his door handle. "It's early enough that we should be able to accomplish everything we want to, but we'd better get started," he said, stepping out of the car and waiting for Ryan to join him.

"Let's go," Ryan said.

As they neared the front entrance of the building, they could hear music blaring from inside. They could smell the stale scent of cigarette smoke that seemed to permeate the air around them.

The bikers standing outside looked at them curiously as they walked closer, studying their clean-shaven faces and the conservativeness of their attire. The suits that Jack and Ryan wore were as out of place in this environment as a fish out of water.

Jack and Ryan flashed their badges as they walked closer to the men, identifying themselves as police officers while questioning them on the identity of the patrons inside the pool hall. Though the men taking up space against the wall were less than cooperative in their responses, the detectives were able to ascertain that four of the people they were looking for were inside. After thanking the men for their time, Jack and Ryan stepped into the building.

Ryan removed his sunglasses as soon as he stepped through the doorway, his eyes taking in the activity around him. Several tables were occupied with friends and acquaintances getting together to make small talk, and the activity by the small stage in a corner indicated that a band was getting set up to play later that night. The majority of people were near the pool tables set up toward the back of the room. Ryan motioned in that direction. "According to that guy we just spoke to, the people at the table in the corner are the ones we need to speak to."

Jack removed his own sunglasses and let his eyes adjust to the dimness of the room. "The tall guy fits the description we have of Carl Taylor. The other three must be his friends. The person outside said you could always find them together in here. Come on," he told Ryan as he began to walk over to where the men stood.

The man they identified as Carl Taylor looked up as they approached, and his eyes narrowed. "Can I help you?" he asked, his eyes scanning over them, as if trying to size them up.

Jack reached for his badge and flashed it. "I'm Detective Reeves, and this is Detective Parks. Are you Carl Taylor?"

The man eyed them suspiciously. "I am."

"Could we have a moment of your time?"

"What's this about?" Carl asked.

"We're investigating a murder. Richard Smythe's," Jack said, watching the man closely as he said the words, looking for any outward sign of unease.

Carl held Jack's gaze for a long moment before he responded with cool composure. "Sure. I can give you a few moments."

"We would appreciate it," Jack said, knowing that the man's curiosity was piqued. He could see it in the questioning way he watched him.

Carl nodded briefly at his words and turned to his companions. "Let me introduce my friends. This is Ralph Jennings, Jake Simms, and Paul Kettle."

Jack inclined his head in greeting before turning his attention back to Carl. "I understand you knew Richard."

Carl picked up his cue stick and took aim at a ball. "Barely," he replied, watching with satisfaction as his ball rolled into a corner pocket. He moved to a different position at the table and took aim at another ball.

"You were involved in a traffic accident with him, weren't you?" Jack asked, realizing that though the man had agreed to talk to them, he wasn't going to be overly cooperative. The way he immediately started playing pool was an indication that getting information from him wasn't going to be easy.

"Several months ago. I didn't have any contact with the guy after that," Carl told him.

"How about his brother? You're a friend of Gary Smythe's, aren't you?" Ryan asked, watching the man's reaction to the name from the corner of his eye.

Carl missed his shot, but other than that, there was no reaction. "More of an acquaintance."

Jack looked over at him. "Really? He said you were at a party he was at yesterday."

Carl shrugged. "So were a lot of people."

"You didn't see much of Gary while you were there?" Ryan asked.

"Nope. Only briefly. He disappeared before the fireworks got started," Carl answered, turning to look at his three companions. "Any of you guys talk to him last night?"

"No," Jake answered.

"Can't say I did," Ralph replied.

"Didn't even lay eyes on him," Paul said.

Carl grimaced and glanced back at Jack and Ryan. "Tough break about Richard Smythe. How did the guy die?"

"Gunshot," Jack said.

Carl winced. "Rough. Sorry about that."

"Maybe you've read about it in the paper this morning," Jack said, instinctively knowing that the man knew more than he let on. Wanting to see what he could find out, he revealed a detail of the murder that wasn't in the paper. "It looked like the result of a break-in. But the funny thing is, it doesn't appear as if anything was stolen," he said, hoping to receive some sort of response. Something that might confirm that the man was aware of what happened.

"I think I did read something about that," Carl acknowledged. "If I remember correctly, the man worked at a brokerage firm."

"That's him," Jack said, looking at Carl suspiciously. The newspaper article that had run on Richard Smythe's murder didn't mention anything about his profession. There hadn't been enough time for the staff writer to get the details of the man's life before the morning edition of the paper had to go to press. The story that ran that morning outlined just the basics, not revealing much of anything about the crime. Jack found it curious that Carl just admitted to knowing two details that hadn't been revealed. For a man that claimed he barely knew Richard Smythe and that he was only an acquaintance of Gary Smythe, he seemed to know an awful lot about Richard. Jack knew it was possible that another one of Gary Smythe's friends had mentioned it in passing, but somehow he doubted it.

Taking a step back, Jack studied the man before him. Though his attire reflected his passion for motorcycles, the man's physical appearance was another matter. Tall, thin, and totally bald, there was an aura about him that hinted at a different lifestyle. One that wasn't dominated by motorcycles and pool halls. He glanced at the man's hands, noticing the manicured fingernails, the pristine cleanliness of the skin, the lack of calluses.

This wasn't a person who worked with his hands, at least not in the same respect as the other men present at the pool hall. If he had to take a guess, he would say that this guy was strictly white collar.

Carl turned his attention back to the pool table. "What exactly do you want from me?" he asked bluntly, resuming his game.

"We're just looking for information. Trying to see if we can come up with anything that will give us a lead in the investigation," Jack replied.

Carl grunted. "Well, I'm sorry I can't be of any assistance, but like I said, I really didn't know Richard."

Jack sensed that he was being dismissed. Carl's sole concentration was now on the game, at least to the casual observer. He couldn't help but notice the slight tenseness in the man's shoulder, and the muscle that was ticking in Carl's jaw. "You were more helpful than you know," Jack assured him, watching as the man's knuckles turned white where they rested on the cue stick.

Ryan looked at the men surrounding the pool table as another ball rolled into a pocket. He removed several business cards from his suit pocket and held them out. "This is the number we can be reached at if you can think of anything that you believe might be helpful with the investigation."

Carl took his time reaching for the card. Glancing at it briefly, he stuck it into his jeans pocket. "Sure, we'll call you," he said before looking over at his companions. "Won't we guys?"

"Yeah," Paul replied.

"Absolutely," Jake said.

"Of course," Ralph answered.

"We appreciate your cooperation," Jack said, knowing instinctively that none of the men would seek them out on their own.

"No problem," Carl replied.

Ryan looked at the four men. "If you hear anything on the street . . ."

"We'll call you," Carl assured him before turning his full attention back to the pool table. "Rack them up," he told Jake.

Ryan and Jack looked at each other, knowing it was time to go. If they wanted more answers, they would have to bring the men in for formal questioning.

"We'll leave you to your game," Jack said, turning to leave, only to notice another man coming over to the table.

"Hey, Carl. Gary is looking for you. He said to tell you that your bike will be ready tomorrow morning at nine," the man said.

The silence that filled the air after the man's remark was deafening, the tension thick enough to slice with a knife. Carl didn't make eye contact with either Jack or Ryan. "Thanks," he muttered.

Chapter Thirteen

The following morning, Jack and Ryan met with Ed in his office to discuss Richard Smythe's murder investigation.

"So what did you two find out last night?" Ed asked, leaning back in his chair and studying them across the expanse of his desk.

Jack stretched his legs out before him. "We tracked down everybody on Gary's list. Nobody claims to know anything that they think might be relevant to the case. From all accounts, the most anybody is claiming is a casual friendship. But there was this one guy on the list, Carl Taylor, who has a little bit of a past with Richard. They were involved in a car accident a few months back. He asserts that was his only connection with him, and he's also stating that his association with Gary is more of an acquaintance than that of friend."

"Carl Taylor?" Ed repeated.

"Yeah," Ryan said, reaching for the small black notebook that he kept in his pocket. Flipping it open, he reviewed his notes. "We asked around last night and found out that he's been hanging around the pool hall for well over a year. His mechanic is Gary Smythe, and he hangs around with the same crowd as Gary."

Ed frowned and tapped his fingers slightly on his desktop. "And he's claiming Gary is just an acquaintance?"

"That's what he's saying. We ran his priors. The guy was arrested a few years back for grand larceny. He cut a deal with the D.A., and never served time," Jack said.

"It doesn't sound as if there's too much there if he was able to cut a deal," Ed replied.

"It gets better," Jack said. "He was also under suspicion for several home burglaries. Burglaries where he gained access to the homes through a window in the basement."

"But the D.A. never got an indictment?" Ed asked.

"He never went for one. They didn't have enough evidence to slam dunk the case, and the witnesses that were ready to testify suddenly had a change of heart. They claimed that they were mistaken in identifying the intruder," Jack answered.

Ed picked up a pen and jotted down a note. "Do you think they were pressured into recanting their statements?"

"Without a doubt," Jack replied.

"By Taylor?" Ed asked.

"We're not sure," Ryan said. "The guy runs with a rough crowd. Any one of his friends could have tried to intimidate the witnesses."

"And, someone was successful," Jack said, reaching for a file that he had brought into the meeting. He took out Carl Taylor's mug shot. "This is a picture of the guy. I thought I would show it to Kayla to see if she's ever seen him around."

"Why would she?" Ed asked, reaching for the picture and studying it. He recalled the sketch their artist had done the night of the murder. Though the drawing bore little resemblance to the photo he now held in his hand, there was a chance that it could have been the same person, if the right alterations were made on his appearance.

"Because he used to work in the mailroom of Richard's brokerage firm," Jack said, removing from the file the preliminary background report that they had been able to obtain.

Ed's eyes shot up to meet his. "What?"

"It was ten years ago. Before Richard accepted a position there," Ryan quickly interjected. "But it's possible that the man kept in touch with a couple of his co-workers after he left. Maybe there's some sort of connection between this guy and Richard's murder."

"We'll have to go down to Richard's office and begin interviewing his associates," Ed said.

"Jack and I will go down there after we speak to Lois and Michael Baker," Ryan assured him. "They're scheduled to be here this morning at ten."

"Do you need my help in obtaining any search warrants?" Ed asked, knowing that they would be needed prior to setting out to avoid any problems or delays.

"Thanks, but I'll take care of it," Jack told him.

Ed. nodded and looked at him. "Let me know if you need me to do anything on my end."

"I will," Jack assured him.

"What about the guy who threw the party Gary Smythe was at on the Fourth? Jimmy Cooper. Did you talk to him?" Ed asked.

"Unfortunately, no," Jack answered. "According to his neighbor, he went on vacation with his family. They left early in the morning on July fifth."

"Where?" Ed questioned.

"Orlando, Florida. He has little kids. She said they were visiting the theme parks," Jack replied.

Ed sighed. "We'll have to talk to him when he gets back."

"We will," Jack assured him.

Ed stared at him for a moment before gesturing to the files on his desk. "I reviewed the background reports that came in. Other than the investigation going on with Michael Baker, there's no real history there. At least nothing that filtered through law enforcement."

"We came to the same conclusion," Ryan replied.

"And the information that came in on Gary Smythe didn't hint at any problems either," Ed said. "The guy looks relatively clean."

"With one exception," Jack injected. "When I met with Kayla yesterday, she said the reason she and Richard couldn't lend money to Lois and Michael was because they had lent it to Gary."

"Which we haven't been able to confirm," Ryan said. "At least, not yet. But we're not through with him. We still need to talk to him about Carl Taylor."

Ed nodded and reached for a couple of faxes on his desk. "I pulled the phone records for Richard Smythe, both residential and cellular."

"And?" Jack prompted.

"There were a couple of calls to the cellular number that we traced to a pay phone at a shopping plaza, but there's no lead there."

"What about the open window in the Smythes' basement? Did they find any prints?" Ryan asked.

"Just Kayla's and Richard's. But if someone used the window to enter or leave the house, and they were wearing gloves, that would explain the lack of additional prints," Ed said, with a quick glance at his watch. "Look, I have a meeting with the D.A. I have to get to. I probably won't see you before you interview the Bakers, so let me know how that goes."

Jack rose to his feet. "Sure, no problem."

"Come to my office after you make your rounds this afternoon. We'll compare notes," Ed said.

Jack nodded and stood before he turned to face Ryan. "We'd better review what we have on the Bakers one final time before we meet with them."

"I'm right behind you," Ryan replied, following Jack out the door.

An hour later, Ryan and Jack sat across from Lois and Michael Baker in a conference room, and their attorney, Robert Greene, was sitting off to the side, ready to interject with legal advice if the situation called for it.

Jack cast a quick look at Ryan before he settled back in his seat and studied the trio before him. Michael Baker looked composed, but Jack didn't miss the slight twitching of his facial muscle as his jaw clenched. It was the only outward sign he gave that he was nervous about the interview. Lois Baker appeared calm, but she constantly shot quick glances at her husband, almost as if she was trying to communicate something without words. And their attorney stared stonily at Jack and Ryan.

Jack knew that the interview that was about to take place was less than ideal. In truth, he would have preferred to meet with both Michael and Lois separately. But meeting together was the one stipulation that the couple had placed on the interview. And it was a stipulation the police weren't in a position to deny. If they had forced separate interviews, he had the feeling that neither Lois nor Michael would have cooperated. It was something that they couldn't risk. They needed answers one way or another. And though Jack sensed that there was a definite reason for them to want to stay together, he couldn't determine if it was strictly for moral support, or if they truly needed to be careful that one didn't implicate the other in the crime.

"We'd like to thank you for agreeing to talk to us," Jack said by way of an opening statement.

Michael Baker looked at his wife briefly and reached out to squeeze her hand. "Believe it or not, we want to help find Richard's murderer. I know it didn't seem that way the other night, but due to circumstances in our lives right now, we'd thought it best to wait until our attorney was present."

"I'm the one who told them not to say anything," Robert Greene said, taking responsibility for the action.

Jack looked at him briefly, but addressed his next comment to Michael and Lois. "I understand that there's a lot going on in your life right now. If the situations were reversed, I might have acted in the same way," he told them in an effort to get them to relax, to let their guard down so that they would talk honestly. Though he didn't fully understand their reluctance to talk the other night, at least not if they didn't have anything to hide, he also knew that people sometimes acted irrationally when under pressure. Right now, he was willing to give them the benefit of the doubt that they truly wanted to help find Richard's killer. He was willing to do that until they proved him wrong.

Michael visibly relaxed at Jack's words. "I appreciate that."

Jack inclined his head in acknowledgment, pleased that his words had the desired effect on the man. "That being said, we need to know what you can tell us about Richard."

Michael released the hold he had on his wife's hand, and folded his own on top of the table. "Such as?"

"Do you know of anybody who would have had a reason to kill him?" Ryan asked bluntly.

Michael didn't hesitate in his reply. "No. And that includes both myself and my wife," he said, automatically answering the unspoken question. "I know you probably heard about the problems I'm having at work. And that Lois and I asked Richard and Kayla for financial assistance. But I assure you, there were no hard feelings when they told us they couldn't help."

"Are you sure about that?" Jack asked.

Lois looked at her attorney briefly before she took it upon herself to answer the question. "He is. I admit, I was a little hurt when Richard and Kayla first refused, but Kayla explained that they just weren't in a position to help us out. She told me about lending money to Gary to buy his house."

"Did she?" Jack questioned, watching her closely, trying to determine the honesty behind her response.

"Yes. After I shamefully accused her of turning her back on her family, she told me about how Gary had come to them for the money just a few weeks before. About how he needed the loan because he had to reinvest his own money into his business. She told me that that if she and Richard hadn't agreed to help Gary financially, it would have taken a toll on Gary's marriage."

Her words were something that Kayla hadn't mentioned when she met with him the day before, and Jack's eyes narrowed slightly. "What exactly do you mean by that?"

"Gary's wife really wanted a house. She was tired of living in an apartment, of renting, and she began resenting that Gary was putting all their money back into his business. I think she was jealous of the attention he gave to his garage. She didn't understand why they weren't able to have the American dream of the house with the picket fence," Lois said.

"I take it she wasn't that involved with the business," Ryan said.

"No. Lisa is a homebody. She enjoys staying at home with the kids. I don't think she ever had any desire to work out of the home. From what Kayla told me, Lisa gave Gary an ultimatum: They either took the plunge and bought a house, or she was going to reevaluate if they wanted the same things in life," Lois replied.

"So Gary went to Richard for the loan," Jack said.

"Yes. And knowing Gary, it had to bother him that he was put in that position. He really hated asking Richard for anything," Lois replied.

"Any idea why?" Ryan asked.

"Because Richard took every opportunity he could to let Gary know that he thought he mishandled his life," Lois said.

Ryan leaned back in his chair as he considered Lois's words. "Could you be a little more specific?"

"I can," Michael said, picking up the conversation where his wife left off. "I played golf on a regular basis with Richard. It was an opportunity for us both to unwind. Needless to say, we used the chance to vent a little about the frustrations in our lives. With me, it was the investigation going on at my office. With Richard, it was how he thought Gary was wasting his life, not living up to his potential. Richard truly believed that Gary should have taken a different path in life. That he should have followed in Richard's footsteps as far as his career. Richard even tried to get Gary a job in his brokerage firm."

"In what capacity?" Jack asked.

"Trainee. Richard thought if he could get him in on the ground floor, Gary would eventually work his way up the ladder," Michael replied.

"How long ago was that?" Ryan asked.

"Just a few months ago, about the time Gary came to him for the loan. I think Richard tried to use that as a bargaining chip before he agreed to lend him the money," Michael said.

"That couldn't have gone over well," Ryan remarked.

"It didn't," Michael replied. "Gary accused Richard of trying to run his life. Of interfering where he had no business."

Jack thought about what Michael had just revealed. "How would you describe their relationship?"

Michael shrugged. "Honestly? I think there was a lot of resentment on Gary's part against Richard. I'm not saying that he didn't love his brother, but the constant hounding to change his life probably took a toll."

"Do you think Richard knew how his brother felt?" Ryan asked.

"I know he did," Michael said. "They got into a huge fight last month over it. I loved Richard like a brother, but I'll be the first to admit that sometimes he just didn't know when to quit. Last month, when we were playing golf one afternoon, he told me he was thinking of calling in the loan he had given Gary unless Gary had a change of heart about going back to school. Richard not only didn't like the direction Gary's life was taking, he wasn't crazy about the people that Gary hung out with."

"Did Richard ever mention specifically which people he had a problem with?" Jack asked.

"No. But I do know that Richard was involved in a car accident a few months back, and the other party had work done by Gary's shop. Richard didn't like that. He wanted Gary to turn away the business," Michael said.

"And Gary refused," Ryan concluded.

"His business isn't going well enough that he can afford to pick and choose his customers," Michael replied.

"You seem to know a lot about the state of Gary's business," Jack observed, watching Michael closely, trying to determine if he was being coached in what he said, if he was trying to deliberately cast suspicion on Richard's brother to take the spotlight off of himself.

Michael shrugged off the observation. "Like I said, Richard and I talked a lot when we played golf together."

Jack nodded slightly and decided to turn the topic of conversation back to Michael and Lois. "Tell me, how is the investigation against yourself progressing? It has to be tough being under a microscope like that."

Michael shifted slightly in his chair, unprepared for the sudden refocus. "I've had better moments. It's not easy staying at home all day. I like to be active. I'm hoping to be cleared soon so that I can start getting my life together. But at least for now, Lois and I can be there for Kayla. She's having a tough time dealing with all this."

"I imagine she is," Jack acknowledged before turning to face Lois. "Kayla had mentioned that you were at a party in the Hamptons the night Richard was murdered."

"Yes," she responded. "I'm involved in several charities on the Island, and one of the chairmen had a party."

Ryan looked at Michael. "You were in attendance too?"

"Yes," Michael replied. "Fortunately, we have some very good friends. They know I'm not capable of doing what Kane Mortgage is accusing me of doing, and they've been very supportive in standing behind us."

"What time did the party start?" Jack asked.

"Around four," Lois answered before looking at her lawyer. "Do you have the list?" she asked him.

Robert took a sheet of paper out of his briefcase. "Right here," he said, handing the paper to Ryan since he was sitting closer.

Ryan reached for the paper and glanced down at it. "This is the guest list of who was in attendance at the party?"

"Yes," Robert answered. "I took the liberty of having my secretary contact the hosts to obtain it. I had a feeling you would want to see it."

"We do, and we appreciate your bringing it," Ryan said.

"My clients want to see justice served. Regardless of first impressions, they have nothing to hide," Robert assured them.

"I'm sure they don't," Ryan replied.

"Do you have any more questions at the moment?" Lois asked.

"Just one," Jack replied.

She looked at him curiously, her body tensing in anticipation. "What?"

"How well did you get along with Richard?" Jack asked.

Lois seemed stunned by the directness of the question. "What do you mean?"

"Your relationship with Richard. How would you categorize it?" Jack clarified, curious about her response. While her husband admitted to being on friendly terms with Richard, something that Kayla had already confirmed, Jack still had a lot of questions about Lois Baker. By all accounts she was a controlling individual. He couldn't help but wonder just how much she clashed with Richard, especially where her sister was concerned.

Lois took her time in responding. "I had nothing against Richard," she hedged.

"That wasn't my question," Jack said, noticing the trouble she was having putting the context of their relationship into words.

Robert Greene looked at Jack. "Exactly what are you asking?"

Jack maintained eye contact with Lois. "I'm asking if Mrs. Baker approved of Richard and Kayla's relationship. If she was on friendly terms with the man."

"Richard was my brother-in-law, and my sister loved

him. Any reservations I may have had about their relationship didn't come into play. I'm not the one who had to live with him," Lois finally responded.

"I take it that means that you and Richard didn't always see eye-to-eye," Jack persisted.

"I really don't believe this questioning is necessary," Robert interjected, only to be cut off by Lois.

Lois glanced briefly at her attorney before turning to face Jack. "It's okay. Detective Reeves wants to know how I felt about Richard. I guess that's a fair question under the circumstances," she said, pausing for a long moment to collect her thoughts.

Jack waited patiently for her to respond. The way she stalled piqued his curiosity in a way that her husband's responses didn't.

"I didn't always approve of the way Richard held my sister back," she finally replied.

"In what way did he hold her back?" Jack asked.

"Her career for one. Before she met Richard, she was a successful interior designer. But once she met Richard, her dreams, the things she needed for fulfillment in her own life took a backseat to his desires and needs. I think he could have been more supportive to her," Lois said.

"And your sister? Did she feel the same way?" Jack persisted.

"She said she didn't, but I know she had to have some resentment. Kayla was asked to design a house out in the Hamptons by one of our friends. She seemed excited when the opportunity presented itself, but the next thing I knew she was turning down the commission. Apparently Richard thought it would interfere with his own promotion. He needed Kayla around for his own rise to the top—dinner parties, office functions—Richard wanted Kayla on his arm at these events. He wanted her help in securing the promotion he recently got," Lois said.

"You sound sure of that," Ryan said, listening intently as she spoke.

Lois laughed, but there was no humor in it. "You searched the house the night of the murder."

"So?" Ryan pressed.

"You must have noticed that they had separate bedrooms. You must have realized that something wasn't right with their relationship," Lois replied.

"And the reason you just gave was the cause for that?" Jack asked.

"Yes," she admitted. "It's something that had been building for a long time, and the separate rooms was a wake-up call to Richard that he needed to start putting Kayla's feelings and needs ahead of his own. They were just starting to come to terms with everything. They were just starting to work things out."

"How do you know?" Ryan asked.

"Kayla told me," she replied, sitting back in her chair.

"Well, thank you for sharing that," Ryan said.

She nodded. "Is there anything else?"

Ryan glanced at Jack briefly before responding. "We'd like to get your fingerprints before you go. It'll help us determine who's been in Richard and Kayla's house."

Lois and Michael were unprepared for the request, and they looked to their attorney for guidance.

"That won't be a problem," Robert answered on their behalf.

"Thank you," Ryan responded.

"Is that it?" Lois asked.

"Yes. But if something comes up, would it be all right if we call you?" Ryan asked.

"Of course," she responded, answering for both her husband and herself. "And if we think of anything that we feel might be useful in Richard's murder investigation, we'll be in touch."

"We would appreciate that," Jack said.

Robert glanced at Jack and Ryan. "I take it this interview is over?"

Jack nodded and stood. "Thank you for your time."

Chapter Fourteen

Later that afternoon, Jack and Ryan were in the Human Resources department at Richard's workplace, waiting to talk to the director, Eric Kline. The modern office building that a security guard had escorted them through was quiet; most of the workers were out to lunch. Those that remained had a somber air about them as they went about their daily activities.

"The employees in the building seem to be feeling the weight of Richard's death," Ryan said, trying to explain the morose atmosphere that seemed to have a hold on the place.

"Yeah, they do, but that's natural. I think everybody who knew the man would have to be feeling something over the fact that he was murdered."

Ryan thought back to the workspaces that they passed. "There didn't appear to be a lot of employees in the building."

"I think Richard had mentioned at one point that this

is just a field office of the brokerage firm. The main office is located in Manhattan."

"Manhattan? Do we have the address? Maybe it'll be worth a trip over to the place. If Richard had a lot of contact with the employees of that office, it's possible that there might be someone there that we should investigate."

"I don't think I saw it noted in any of the reports we pulled, but we should be able to get it before we leave here today," Jack said just as the door to the office opened.

Both Jack and Ryan turned and watched as a tall, well-dressed man with silver hair entered the room.

"Detectives? I'm Eric Kline. I understand you wanted to see me," he said as he walked over to his desk to take a seat.

Jack immediately reached out to shake the man's hand. "Mr. Kline. I'm Detective Reeves and this is Detective Parks. We appreciate you taking the time to talk to us."

"It's not a problem," Eric replied, motioning to the two chairs in front of his desk. "Please, take a seat. The security guard mentioned that this was in regard to Richard Smythe's death."

"That's correct. We were wondering if you would be able to shed any light on the man."

"I'll try to be of assistance," Eric assured them. "But first, could you tell me exactly what kind of information you're looking for?"

"We'd like to know what Richard's relationships with his co-workers were like," Ryan said.

"His relationships? I guess they were okay," Eric said.

Jack probed a little deeper into the vague response. "Do you know if Richard had any enemies here at the firm?"

"Not that I'm aware of. I'm sure there were the normal types of resentments going on about his getting the promotion, but that's fairly typical in any firm. If you're asking if I think anybody would have had cause to kill the man, I'm afraid I wouldn't be able to help you. As far as I know, Richard was on fairly friendly terms with everybody here."

"You said normal types of resentment," Jack said, his attention grabbed by the turn of phrase. "Could you be more specific? Are we talking about professional rivalry?"

"Well, yes, but as I said, that's fairly common. People often try to outdo each other in the workplace. It's a way of getting attention, of being acknowledged."

"Were there any particular instances where this occurred?" Ryan asked.

"I could think of one offhand. It was before Richard received his latest promotion. There were a couple of people being considered for it: Tad Jenkins and Maureen Harris. Both were qualified for the position."

"Did they express any discord when Richard was appointed Vice President?" Ryan questioned.

"No. As a matter-of-fact, I know they both wished him well. We had a celebration dinner for Richard and all the employees at the firm attended. I would think that if any one of them held a real grudge against Richard, they would have stayed away."

"Are Tad Jenkins and Maureen Harris here today?" Ryan asked.

"I'm afraid not. Tad's been working out of the

Manhattan office for the last couple of weeks. He's actually expressed an interest in making a transfer to that location. And Maureen went on vacation a couple of days before the Fourth. She's in California visiting family."

"Do you have any way we could reach them to talk to them?" Ryan asked.

"Are they under suspicion?"

"Right now, we're just looking for information," Ryan replied, bypassing the question entirely.

"I guess that makes sense," Eric replied, reaching for his Rolodex. Shifting through the cards it contained, he made a note of the phone numbers he had for Tad and Maureen on the back of his own business card and handed it to Ryan. "Here're their company cell phone numbers. They're pretty good about answering their calls, so you should have no problem reaching them. If they ask how you got the numbers, please let them know that I gave them to you."

Ryan glanced briefly at the card before he pocketed it, noticing that it had the address and main phone number for both office locations of the brokerage firm. "You're the director of Human Resources for both offices?"

"I am."

"So you have access to everyone's personnel file?"

"Yes. If you need any information on anyone, I would be the one you would see."

"Then we may be talking to you again," Ryan said.

"I'll try and be of assistance in any way I can."

"Thanks."

"It's not a problem."

"There is something else that we'd like to discuss

with you," Jack said, reaching for the file he had brought with Carl Taylor's photo. He pulled it out and handed it to Eric. "Does this man look familiar?"

Eric reached for the photograph and studied it. "Sure. That's Carl Taylor. He worked here about ten years ago."

"How long was he employed for?" Jack asked.

"A little over a year," Eric replied, handing back the photo. "He was a good worker. I'm sorry we had to lose him."

"Why did he leave?" Ryan asked.

"He was only working here temporarily. His cousin got him the job while he took a year off from attending school."

Jack frowned. "His cousin?"

"Yes. Randy Johnson. He worked in our accounting department for over fifteen years."

"Does he still work here?" Jack asked, wondering if they would get the opportunity to speak with the man.

"I'm afraid not. He passed away about five years back. Heart attack."

"I'm sorry," Jack said.

Eric inclined his head in appreciation of the words. "We all were. He had a massive heart attack while at work. There was nothing the paramedics could do for him."

"That's a tough break," Ryan sympathized.

"Yes," Eric agreed. "Actually, Richard was with the man at the time."

"They were friends?" Jack questioned.

"I wouldn't exactly say that. Unfortunately, it was during a staff meeting where they were announcing a new position in the finance department. Both Richard and Randy were up for the job."

"And Richard got it," Jack concluded.

"Yes. Carl was very close to his cousin. I know he took the death hard," Eric admitted.

"Did Carl know Richard?" Jack asked, knowing that they were just given a possible motive for Carl Taylor to kill Richard.

"I'm not sure how well they knew each other. Carl was already gone from the company by the time Richard joined us. I recall seeing them speak together at Randy's funeral, but I couldn't tell you if that was due to the fact that they did know one another, or if it was due to the circumstances," Eric replied, unaware of the direction Jack's thoughts had gone.

"Was it ever determined what caused the heart attack?" Ryan asked.

"Not really, at least nothing that was revealed to us. I know Randy was under a lot of stress during the weeding out process for the position, but in all fairness, all of the employees applying for the post were. It was a little cutthroat around here during that time as each of the possible candidates tried to prove themselves. It's unfortunate that it took the toll on Randy that it did."

"Yes, it is," Jack agreed, moving the photo back into the folder. "If it's okay with you, we'd like to speak with the employees here today, just to get an idea if they know of anyone that may have had an issue with Richard. If they're aware of any problems that we should investigate."

"Of course," Eric replied, reaching for his phone.

"I'll call the guard booth and have them set up one of the conference rooms for you to use. It'll be easier that way. People should be returning from lunch any moment now, so you should get the opportunity to speak to just about everyone."

"We appreciate your help," Ryan assured him.

"It's not a problem."

It was a couple of hours later before Jack and Ryan finished interviewing Richard's co-workers. Most of them wanted to be of assistance, a few of them didn't want to get involved, but over all, the process went well. They were able to determine that nobody currently working at the firm held any real grudge against Richard, and that included both Tad Jenkins and Maureen Harris. Ryan had made contact with the two of them while Jack spoke to the other employees present, and there was no indication that either of them had anything to do with Richard's death.

As Jack and Ryan walked out to the car, Jack's cell phone rang.

"Reeves," he said, answering the summons.

"Jack, it's Ashley."

"Hi, babe. What's up?"

"I was wondering if you could stop by the house."

"Is something wrong?" Jack immediately asked.

"No. Everything's fine," she assured him. "It's just that Kayla's here, and she's upset."

Jack frowned at Ashley's words. "Why?"

"She came over to her house to get some clothes, and I guess going back into the house was too much for her. I found her sitting on her front step, crying. I don't know what to do to help her. She's in our living room now trying to pull herself together, but she's having a tough time."

Jack cast a quick glance at his watch. "Ryan and I can be there in twenty minutes," he said, calculating the time it would take to make the drive, while in the back of his mind wondering if something else happened.

"All right. In the meantime, I'll see if I can get her to open up a little bit," Ashley said.

"I'll see you soon," Jack promised, disconnecting the call.

"Who was that?" Ryan asked as soon as Jack broke the connection.

"Ashley. Kayla Smythe's at the house and she's crying. Ashley's not sure what to do for her."

"Is this the first time she's been to her house since the night of the shooting?" Ryan asked.

"As far as I know."

"Then maybe everything is catching up with her."

"Maybe. But regardless, we should talk to her," Jack said, opening the car door and getting into the driver's side.

Ryan slid into the car and automatically reached for the seat belt. "We were going to stop by and see her later to see if she could identify the photograph of Carl Taylor. This will give us the chance to see if she can connect him to Richard."

"Yeah, and I have to admit, I am curious about that. Especially after Eric Kline mentioned that Richard got the position that Taylor's cousin was up for. The deeper into the investigation we get, the more this guy appears to show up."

"Well, hopefully Kayla will be able to shed some light on it."

"We'll know soon enough," Jack said, starting the engine.

Chapter Fifteen

Ashley and Kayla were sitting in the living room when Jack and Ryan arrived at the house.

"Hi," Jack greeted as he walked into the room, his gaze taking in the stress that was outlined on Ashley's face before his focus shifted to Kayla. He noticed the stark paleness of her complexion, the red-rimmed eyes that indicated she had recently been crying. Though it was obvious that she was visibly upset, she seemed to have the worst under control.

"Hi," Ashley replied, rising from the sofa to greet him before looking over at Ryan. "Hi, Ryan."

"Hi, Ashley," Ryan replied, standing a little awkwardly from the situation he found himself in. He didn't know what to say to Kayla. Jack and Ashley knew the woman, he didn't. Other than interviewing her the night of the murder, he had never met her before. And while he was curious about what had gotten her so upset that day, he knew instinctively that it would have to be Jack who made the first attempt at conversation with the woman.

Ashley sensed Ryan's discomfort and she gave him a small smile of encouragement before she turned to look over at Kayla. "I'm going to go and put on a fresh pot of coffee. Jack will keep you company while I'm gone."

Kayla looked as if she was going to protest at being left alone, but she caught herself before the objection left her lips. Instead she nodded, and glancing in Jack's direction, she offered him an apology. "I'm sorry about this, Jack."

Jack smiled at her sympathetically. "You have nothing to apologize for," he assured her as he walked over to the sofa and took a seat beside her. "How are you holding up?" he asked her gently.

Kayla expelled a ragged breath. "Okay. It was just so hard going into the house today. I didn't expect it to be that difficult."

Jack nodded in understanding. "Is there anything Ashley or I could do for you to make this a little easier?"

"No, but thanks for offering. I need to get used to going into the house. I can't stay with my sister forever."

"I'm sure she's not rushing you to leave," Jack said.

"She's not," Kayla agreed, her gaze downcast. "But eventually I'd like my life to return to normal."

"I can understand that," Jack replied, knowing that the woman had to be feeling as if she was in some sort of limbo. What she was going through had to be torture.

"You talked with Lois and Michael today," Kayla said.

"Yes," Jack responded, though her words were more of a statement than a question.

"How did it go?"

"It went well," Jack assured her. "They were very cooperative."

She nodded. "I knew they would be," she said, her eyes shifting to Ryan who still stood in the entryway to the room.

Jack followed her gaze. "Kayla, you remember my partner Ryan from the other night, don't you?" he asked, looking over at Ryan and gesturing him to have a seat. He had a feeling that Ryan's hovering was making Kayla nervous, and he wanted to put her at ease.

"Of course," she said, visibly relaxing as she recalled meeting him that night. "Hello."

"Hi," Ryan replied, walking over and taking a seat across from the sofa where Jack and Kayla sat.

After Ryan was settled, Jack turned his attention back to Kayla. "You had mentioned your sister and brother-in-law. Did you talk to them after they met with us today?"

"Yes. They were glad that they had the opportunity to speak with you."

Jack didn't exactly get that impression, but he didn't correct her. For the most part, the Bakers were being cooperative. He couldn't exactly blame them if they were a little leery of the police considering the investigation going on with Michael. "Could I ask you something?"

"Sure."

"Michael mentioned that Richard had made some comments during one of their golf outings about Gary, and the direction his life was going. Did Richard ever say anything to you about it?"

"No," she answered without hesitation. "I knew Gary

was having problems both in his marriage and financially, but that was the extent of what Richard told me."

"Do you have any idea of why Richard would talk to Michael and not yourself?" Ryan asked.

"Because Richard thought it was his job to protect me from things like that. Richard had some very old-fashioned views on women and their role in society. To be honest, he handled all of our financial concerns, all of our legal papers, everything. I guess that was part of the problem today."

"Meaning?" Jack prompted.

She shrugged helplessly. "It's bad enough going into the house where Richard was murdered. But now I have to start putting things together. I have to make the funeral arrangements, notify the banks, take care of our life insurance policies. It's a bit overwhelming."

"I'm sure it is," Jack sympathized, getting his first real indication of just how much Richard kept Kayla cocooned, of how dependent she would have been on the man. It was something that was rare in this day and age. "Kayla, we have a photograph of someone that we'd like you to look at. Would you mind?"

"Of course not."

"Ryan?" Jack prompted.

Ryan reached for the folder that he had brought into the house. Opening the cover, he removed the photograph of Carl Taylor and handed it to Kayla. "Do you recognize this man?"

Kayla took the photo and studied it for a moment. "He looks familiar."

"Familiar how? Do you remember where you saw him before?" Jack asked, his eyes narrowing slightly as he waited for her to answer.

"I can't be sure, but I think it was at Gary's daughter's christening," she said.

"He's a friend of Gary's?" Ryan pushed.

"I guess so. I don't know why else he would have been at the church or the party afterward."

"Did you see Richard talk to him that day?" Jack asked.

She shook her head and handed back the photograph. "No, but there were a lot of people there. I guess it's possible that he did and I just didn't notice it. Why are you asking?"

"He's just someone we're interested in speaking with," Jack said, deliberately leaving out that the man was a person of interest in Richard's murder.

"Gary could probably tell you more," she told him.

"We were going to stop by and talk to him this afternoon," Jack revealed.

Kayla grimaced. "He's a little upset with me at the moment. I think I hurt his feelings when I didn't call him the night of Richard's murder."

"Things always get a little complicated when emotions are involved," Jack sympathized.

"Yeah, they do," Kayla agreed. "To be honest, it just never occurred to me to call him that night. We weren't that close."

"But he was close to Richard?" Ryan asked.

"They were brothers," she said as if that explained everything.

"Coffee's ready," Ashley said, interrupting their conversation. Her eyes met Jack's. "Everything okay?"

"Yeah," Jack assured her.

Ashley smiled and turned to Kayla. "Tell me what you need me to do to help, and I'll gladly do it."

"Thanks, but I'm okay now. I think the pressure of everything just came to a head before. I didn't mean to have a meltdown in front of you," Kayla replied.

"If you can't have a meltdown in front of friends, who can you do it in front of?" Ashley kidded, trying to relieve some of the tension. She knew it wasn't helping the woman to have everybody so focused on her. She needed to come to terms with everything in her own time, in her own way.

"I appreciate your support," Kayla told her.

"I'm just glad we're here for you," Ashley replied, setting the tray down on the coffee table and pouring the beverage into the cups.

"None for me, thanks," Ryan told Ashley when he noticed the four cups that rested on the tray.

"Jack?" Ashley asked.

"No, thanks. We should probably head out. We have a lot we need to take care of today," Jack said, turning to look once more at Kayla. "Unless you'd like me to go over to your house with you?"

Kayla immediately declined the offer. "Thanks, but it's not necessary. It'll probably be better if I adjust on my own."

"Are you sure? I don't mind going over there with you," Jack assured her.

"I'm sure."

"All right. But if you need me for anything, just call Ashley. She knows how to reach me," Jack said.

Kayla smiled slightly. "Thanks."

Jack nodded and turned to Ashley. "Ryan and I are going to leave. Do you need anything before we go?"

"Actually, if you could stop at the store and pick up some baby formula on the way home tonight, it would be a big help. John's sleeping right now, but he should be getting up shortly. He's been a little fussy today, so I really don't think it would be a good idea for me to take him out."

"Is he okay?" Jack immediately asked.

"Yes," Ashley assured him. "It's just one of those days."

Jack smiled. "I'll pick up the formula. Do we need anything else?"

"Something for dinner?"

"Any preferences?"

"Pizza's fine with me if it's okay with you."

"Sure. Not a problem."

Ashley smiled at him. "Thanks."

"I'll see you later."

Chapter Sixteen

Ryan turned to speak to Jack as soon as they left the house. "Kayla seemed okay. Based on what Ashley said to you, I thought she was going to be more of an emotional wreck."

"Yeah, I know. I thought so too. She seems to be handling things fairly well considering the circumstances."

"Let me ask you something. Did you find it strange that Richard would have mentioned things to Michael about his brother that he didn't mention to Kayla?" Ryan asked.

"I don't know if strange is the word I would use. Kayla hit it on the head when she labeled him as old-fashioned. But I didn't know either of them well enough to draw any conclusions on that point."

Ryan grunted. "So, who do you want to go and visit first—Gary Smythe or Carl Taylor?"

"Since Kayla mentioned she thought she saw Carl Taylor at Gary's daughter's christening, let's start with

Gary. I'm curious if he'll say that the man is just an acquaintance, or if he'll put more importance on the relationship."

"Sounds good to me," Ryan said, reaching up to adjust his sunglasses against the harsh glare of the sun.

"Then let's get out of here."

Thirty minutes later, Jack parked the car in the lot across the street from the garage that Gary Smythe owned. The place was crawling with people, and cars and motorcycles were backed up into the street as they waited to be serviced.

Ryan watched the activity going on. "Business doesn't look like it's hurting," he observed.

"No, it doesn't. Do you recall when Gary opened the shop? I know the first few years of any new venture are tough. It's possible that Gary's financial problems are stemming from trying to get the business off the ground."

"I think our report said that he owned the shop for a little over three years. Before that, he worked here as a mechanic."

"Three years could still put the business in a make-or-break mode."

"True," Ryan agreed. "But if the amount of traffic in and out of this place is any indication, Gary should have a firm foothold with his customers."

Jack looked over at him. "Before we go in there, why don't you call the station and have them see if they can pull Gary's financial records. When we meet with Ed tonight, we can review everything and see if the information the Bakers gave us about Gary's financial status holds any water."

"Sure," Ryan said, reaching for the cell phone to place the call. When he was through, he looked at Jack. "They promised they're going to work on it this afternoon."

"Good. Then let's go see if Gary can shed any more light on this mess," Jack said, opening his car door and stepping out into the hot and sunny afternoon.

"I'm right behind you," Ryan replied.

They found Gary in a small windowed office working on paperwork. The glass window of the office allowed a full view of the mechanics on duty as they worked on the vehicles, yet provided some reprieve from the noise of the tools.

Jack knocked once on the glass panel of the door before entering the small room. "Mr. Smythe?"

Gary looked up at the interruption, the mask of concentration that had been on his face only moments earlier all but disappearing. "Detectives, have you found out something about my brother's death?" he immediately asked, turning his full attention on them.

"I'm afraid not. Right now, we just need to ask you a few more questions if we could," Jack replied. "Do you have a moment?"

"Of course. Come in," Gary invited.

"Thanks," Jack said, entering the enclosure and waiting for Ryan to do the same before closing the door.

Gary waved them to a couple of vacant seats. "Have a seat."

Jack moved over to a chair. "You have a thriving business going here," he acknowledged.

"It's been a tough road, but it's getting there," Gary responded proudly before changing the subject to the reason behind their visit. "So tell me, what can I help you with?"

Jack thought about the best way to broach the subject of Gary's loan from Richard and Kayla, and he realized there was no easy way to bring it up. If he wanted answers, he was going to have to come right out and ask. "We came across some information that suggested you borrowed money from your brother for the down payment of a house."

Gary showed no emotional response to the comment. His answer was very matter-of-fact. "That's right."

"Did Richard ever put any type of stipulations on your request to borrow the money?" Jack asked.

"Stipulations?" Gary repeated. "What do you mean?"

"Did he ever try to use the loan as a bargaining tool for you to change your lifestyle?" Jack clarified bluntly, hoping that the forthright question wouldn't put Gary on the defensive.

"Of course not," Gary denied vehemently. "Richard would never do that."

"Are you sure?" Ryan asked, stepping into the conversation.

"Positive," Gary assured them, swiveling in his desk chair to a filing cabinet and opening a drawer. He rifled through several folders before he pulled out the document that he was looking for. "This is a copy of our agreement," he said, handing over the paper for their review.

Jack reached for the document and read it before passing it over to Ryan. "You had an attorney draw up paperwork for the loan?"

"I wasn't looking for a handout. To be honest, I didn't even want to borrow the money. I didn't think it was necessary. But my wife really wanted this house that was on the market, and the timing was bad. Richard was the one who offered me the loan," Gary said.

"At no interest," Ryan murmured, handing back the document.

"At no interest," Gary confirmed. "Just out of curiosity, who told you that Richard put a stipulation on the loan? Was it Kayla?"

"No, it wasn't Kayla," Jack answered, seeing no harm in revealing that piece of information. He didn't want to leave the man with the wrong impression. He didn't want to put any more of a strain on the man's relationship with his sister-in-law than what already existed.

"You're not going to tell me who it was," Gary guessed correctly.

"Right now, who said what isn't relevant. Our only concern is to get to the bottom of who murdered your brother," Jack replied.

"On that I agree with you wholeheartedly," Gary said.

"Then maybe you can answer another question for us," Jack said.

"What's that?" Gary asked.

"We need to know what your association is with Carl Taylor," Jack said, watching Gary closely.

"My association? I guess I consider him a friend. I do a lot of business for the guy, and he's been decent about paying his bills on time."

"How often do you see him?" Ryan pressed.

"I see him fairly frequently at friends' houses. As a matter-of-fact, he was staying with one of my close friends during the time of my daughter's christening. My wife felt funny about him staying home alone while my friend came to the christening, so she invited him along. He seemed to appreciate the invitation," Gary replied.

"Carl Taylor's the person who got into an accident with Richard, wasn't he?" Jack asked.

"Yeah. Richard didn't care for the man, but that could have been because the guy damaged Richard's new sports car. I guess if the situations were reversed, I would feel the same way."

"Did Carl Taylor ever mention anything about your brother to you?" Ryan asked, curious about the answer.

"No. I mean I felt some tension when the two of them met at my daughter's christening, but nothing that indicated that they had major issues with each other," Gary said.

"Did Richard ask you not to work on Carl Taylor's vehicles any more?" Jack questioned.

"Yeah, he did. But it was after he had the accident. He was upset at the time. I didn't put any credence on it, and I don't think Richard really expected me to. He knew I wasn't in a position to turn down business. He would have been the last one who would have wanted me to."

"Richard was very astute at business," Jack agreed, thinking about the document that Gary had showed them willingly. The amount of money stipulated, the repayment terms which were pretty much open-ended, and the no interest clause all supported the theory that Richard cared deeply for his brother. Yet by all accounts, the information they had obtained on Richard showed that the man could be controlling. Gary had admitted as much in the very first interview after Richard's death. But Richard's using the loan as a tool to force his brother to change his life didn't make sense. Not after Jack saw the volume of business Gary's shop was doing. If nothing else, Richard was a businessman. He would have seen that the shop was a successful venture.

Gary's gaze encompassed both Jack and Ryan. "Did you have any further questions for me?"

"No, I think you addressed all of our concerns for the moment," Jack replied, rising to his feet. "Thanks for taking the time to meet with us."

"It's not a problem," Gary assured them. "If you need anything else clarified, let me know."

"We will," Jack said.

"Can you see yourselves out?" Gary asked.

"Sure," Jack replied. "We'll be in touch if anything surfaces in your brother's investigation."

"Thanks," Gary replied.

"We'll talk to you soon," Jack said, walking out of the office with Ryan following close behind.

"What did you think?" Ryan asked the moment they cleared the garage and were out of earshot of all the workers.

"The man seemed very cooperative," Jack replied. "He didn't look like he was trying to hide anything. He pulled out that agreement on the loan with no prompting from us."

"True."

"And there's one thing that he said that makes sense. Richard would recognize a good business opportunity when he saw one. I don't see him trying to force Gary to change careers midstream when the business was doing well—at least by outward appearances."

"I thought the same thing. But then the question arises, how truthful was Michael Baker being when he spoke with us this morning?"

"It could just be that he misinterpreted some of Richard's comments. By Gary's own remarks during the first interview, Richard had some reservations about Gary's lifestyle. Maybe he just vocalized those objections to Michael, and Michael put his own spin on it."

"Maybe," Ryan agreed.

"But regardless, we'll have to sort through that a little later. Right now, I want to head over to Carl Taylor's apartment and talk to him one more time."

"Did you bring the warrant?"

"I have it."

"Then let's get it over with."

Chapter Seventeen

A short while later, Jack parked the car by the curb of the two-story apartment house where Carl Taylor lived. Shutting the engine, he glanced at the brick structure before him. Though the building was obviously old, it was well maintained. The white wooden shutters against the windows boasted a new coat of paint, and the grass and shrubs had been recently trimmed.

Ryan released his seat belt catch. "It looks like a decent place to live," he observed as he inspected the grounds.

"Yeah, it does," Jack agreed, reaching for his door handle. "Didn't our report state that the man would be home today?" he asked, thinking back to the report they had been able to pull on Carl's latest job as an accountant at a small electronics company.

"So his supervisor said."

"It doesn't look like he's here," Jack said, finding no evidence that the man was home. The blinds were closed tightly against the afternoon sun, and no vehicles were parked in the assigned spaces in front of the building.

"Maybe he had other things to take care of," Ryan suggested, reaching for his own door handle.

Jack closed his car door and headed up the walk. "There's one way to find out," he said as he stopped at the door and raised a hand to knock on the wood.

"Can I help you gentlemen?" a woman's voice asked from above.

Jack took a step back and glanced up, catching sight of a woman with short brown curly hair looking down at them from the apartment on the second floor. He took out his badge and flashed it. "Police, ma'am. We're looking for the gentleman who lives in this apartment. Would you happen to know where he is?"

"Carl?" she asked.

"Carl Taylor," Jack told her, watching her eyes narrow as she studied them from above.

"Stay right there," she ordered, stepping back from the window.

Ryan glanced at Jack. "Do you think she knows anything on his whereabouts?" he asked.

"I don't know. But we'll soon find out," Jack murmured as he heard the woman's footsteps descending the stairs.

It wasn't long before the door next to Carl Taylor's opened and the woman appeared in the doorway. She looked at Jack and Ryan suspiciously. "What do the police want with Carl?" she asked bluntly.

"It's official business Ms. . . ." Jack said, sidestepping the question while opening the dialogue for her to reveal her name.

"Mrs. Taylor."

"Any relation to Carl Taylor?" Jack asked.

"He's my son," she admitted slowly, as if she wasn't sure if it was something she should reveal.

Jack managed to contain his surprise. "Do you know where your son is at the moment?"

"What do you want with him?" she persisted, evading his question.

Jack realized that she wasn't going to answer any questions until they did. Reaching into his jacket, he pulled out the search warrant they had obtained for Carl Taylor's residence. "We have a warrant to search his apartment."

"May I see it?" she asked, holding out a hand.

"Why?" Ryan asked.

"Because I own this building. If you have a warrant to search any part of this property, I have a right to confirm that."

Jack's eyes met Ryan's briefly before he handed over the document. He watched as she donned a pair of reading glasses that hung from around her neck and carefully read it. When she was through, she removed the glasses and let them fall back to her chest.

"Well?" Jack prompted.

She nodded. "I don't know where my son is, but if you give me a moment, I'll go and get the key to his door."

"Thank you," Jack said.

Ryan watched as she entered her own apartment. "Do you think he's in her place?"

"I doubt it. Neither one of them knew we were coming. There would have been no reason for him to hide out there."

"Still . . ." Ryan murmured, watching the doorway to

the woman's apartment, waiting for her to come back down. He didn't have to wait long.

"Here we go," Mrs. Taylor said as she walked over to her son's apartment and unlocked the door. She immediately reached for a light switch on the inside wall, and then stepped aside so that they could enter. "What exactly are you looking for?" she asked, watching them closely.

"We'll let you know when we find it," Jack responded, stepping around the woman to begin his search. The whole time he was conscious of her hovering anxiously in the background. "What time did you see your son last?" he asked as he opened a desk drawer and began searching the contents.

"Last night around six. We had dinner together."

"And you have no idea where he went today?" Ryan asked, walking through the living room and into the hallway to open the linen closet. He immediately began shuffling through the items on the top shelf, noticing the different paraphernalia that the man kept.

"No. Carl always gets up earlier than me. It's not unusual for him to take off on his day off."

"Are there any particular places that he likes to go?" Jack questioned.

"He likes to ride his bike upstate. It's quiet up there and he likes that. It gives him a chance to think."

"About what?" Jack asked, noticing that Ryan had moved into the bedroom to continue the search. He heard the dresser drawers open as Ryan rifled through the contents, and he noticed that the woman instinctively took a step in that direction.

Casually, so he wouldn't alarm her, he stepped in

front of her path, effectively blocking her intrusion into the room. "You never answered my question," he said softly, trying to keep any hint of threat from his voice. He didn't want to frighten her, he just wanted to give Ryan the opportunity to search the rest of the apartment without her interfering.

She glanced at him briefly, her attention momentarily diverted back to him. "What question?"

"What does your son think about on his bike rides?"

"I couldn't answer that," she said, trying to look around him to see what Ryan was doing.

Jack once again shifted his body so that he blocked her path. "He never mentioned anything that was bothering him lately?"

"No," she insisted, becoming impatient with the questions.

"Are you sure?"

"Yes."

"When he leaves for his bike rides, how long does he usually stay out for?" Jack continued to question.

"He's usually back by nightfall."

"Always? Does he ever stay out all night?"

"No. He doesn't like to leave me alone. Carl helps me run the apartment complex. He takes care of the books."

"Has he always done that?"

"Ever since high school. He's always had a head for business."

Jack looked at Ryan as he walked out of the bedroom and over to where he stood. He couldn't help but notice that Ryan carried several pieces of paper in his hand. "What did you find?"

"Take a look," Ryan said, handing over the information he had uncovered in the man's bedroom.

Jack frowned and reached for the documents, surprised to find several newsletters from Richard's company that referred to Richard's promotion. Richard's name was highlighted with a yellow marker. Looking through the papers he held, Jack also noticed a copy of the police report from the accident Carl and Richard had been involved in.

"Look at the dates on the newsletters," Ryan urged.

Jack glanced down at the documents and immediately looked at the dates. They covered a wide period. There were a couple from when the man's cousin, Randy Johnson, worked at the firm, but most were more recent, including one from a week ago.

"What's that?" Mrs. Taylor questioned, automatically trying to catch a glimpse of what Jack held in his hand.

Jack avoided the question and handed the items back to Ryan. "Why don't you call Ed and see if you can get some backup out here so that we can do a thorough search. I'm going to take Mrs. Taylor outside to explain a little bit about what's going on and what we're going to be doing here this afternoon."

"Sure," Ryan said.

"Mrs. Taylor? Why don't you come with me and I'll see if I can shed some light on this for you," Jack told her, escorting her out the front door.

Chapter Eighteen

Several hours later, Jack and Ryan were back at the police station meeting with Ed in his office, discussing the evidence uncovered at Carl Taylor's apartment.

Ed tapped the newsletters safely encased in a paper envelope with this index finger. "Every one of these newsletters references Richard Smythe."

"And a few of them are from the period of time when Carl Taylor's cousin, Randy Johnson, worked at the firm," Jack pointed out.

Ed reached for another piece of evidence that had been uncovered. "This is a copy of the police report from the night Carl Taylor was involved in the car accident with Richard."

"The papers were found together," Ryan revealed. "And that contradicts Carl Taylor's statement that he barely knew Richard."

"Which puts him in the spotlight as a suspect in Richard Smythe's murder. There's only one reason a person would lie in a case like this, and that's if they had something to hide that they knew would implicate them in the crime." Ed motioned to the evidence on his desk. "These are the only items you were able to uncover at Taylor's residence?"

"Everything there links him to Richard Smythe," Jack said.

"What's the connection between Randy Johnson and this case?" Ed questioned.

"The man was in line for another position at the company at the same time as Richard, but Richard got the promotion. Shortly afterward, Randy Johnson died of a heart attack. Richard was with him at the time," Jack replied.

Ed's brow wrinkled in a frown as he thought about Jack's words. "You think Taylor held Richard responsible for that?"

"I'm not sure. Stranger things have happened."

"That's true," Ed acknowledged. "You said Taylor's mother owns the apartment building where he lives and she was there when you searched the place. Did you ask her if she knew why her son would have copies of the newsletters from the firm where Richard worked?"

Jack shrugged. "She claims that she doesn't know anything. She offered the explanation that her son has several friends still employed at the firm. She believes that he only had the recent documents because one of those people gave it to him. She didn't think it was unusual since he worked there himself ten years ago."

Ed's eyebrows lifted. "And how did she explain the articles on Richard where his name had been highlighted?"

"She didn't," Jack replied.

"How did she react when you two showed up with the warrant?" Ed asked.

"She was suspicious," Ryan admitted. "But she didn't do or say anything that was out of line. If I had to categorize it, I would say that she wasn't totally surprised by us showing up at the man's apartment."

"And since Taylor's had some problems with the law in the past . . ." Jack added, letting the words speak for themselves.

"There's probably not a lot that surprises her," Ed finished. He paused for a moment before asking, "Was she cooperative at least?"

"To a certain extent," Jack said. "If you're asking if she went out of her way to volunteer any information, then the answer would be no. If you're asking if she hedged any of our direct questioning, she gave the impression that she was willing to answer the questions as long as she knew her answers wouldn't directly implicate her son with any crimes."

Ed sat back in his chair and contemplated the evidence before him. "I want to bring this guy in for formal questioning. I think we have enough here to issue an arrest warrant, and I want to have that ready if we don't like the man's answers."

"We already informed his mother that we wanted to speak with him," Ryan said.

Ed looked over at Ryan, a slight frown marring his features. "Do you think that was wise?"

Ryan lifted a shoulder in a shrug. "Time will tell. The woman's not stupid. She would have to know that her son would be brought in for formal questioning just from our appearance at his apartment."

"She had no idea where Taylor went? She had no way of contacting him?" Ed questioned.

"So she says. She insists that he never stays away all night," Jack said before suggesting, "We should post an officer outside the apartment building in case he comes back and decides to head out again."

"Do you expect him to run?" Ed asked.

"Right now, I'm not sure what to expect. From everything we've been able to uncover, the man seemed to have a problem with Richard. Whether or not it was a big enough problem to kill him remains to be seen," Jack said.

Ed jotted down a note. "I'll take care of assigning an officer to watch the outside of Taylor's residence." He laid down his pen. "You guys also spoke with Gary Smythe today, didn't you?"

Jack inclined his head. "Yeah. Also Kayla Smythe."

"You went to the Bakers' residence?" Ed asked, surprised to hear that they had met with the woman.

"It wasn't necessary. She was with Ashley."

"Visiting?"

"No. From what I could gather, today was the first time she went back to her own house since the night her husband was murdered. I guess the stress was too much for her, and Ashley found her sitting on the front porch step crying. She invited her back to our place and called me," Jack said.

Ed didn't show any reaction to Jack's statement. "Did you get the chance to show her the picture of Carl Taylor?"

"Yeah, and she seemed to recognize him from Gary Smythe's daughter's christening."

"Was she able to corroborate anything that her sister and brother-in-law stated earlier?" Ed asked.

Jack expelled a small sigh. "She claims that Richard didn't discuss anything about his brother with her."

"Do you believe her?"

"We have nothing to refute the claim."

Ed was silent for a moment. "So we can't even be sure if Michael Baker was being truthful, or if he was trying to throw up a smoke screen. What about Gary Smythe? What was he like when you met with him earlier?"

"There was a big difference in his demeanor when we met with him today than from the other morning," Ryan said.

"In what way?" Ed asked, leaning back in his chair.

"He was more sure of himself. He didn't seem like he had anything to hide. As a matter-of-fact, he was very forthcoming. When we asked him about the money that Richard and Kayla lent him, he willingly showed us a copy of the agreement his attorney drew up. He stated that there was no pressure from Richard regarding any type of repayment on the loan."

"Which refutes Michael Baker's claim."

"Did Gary Smythe's financial records come in?" Ryan asked.

"No. The computers were down this afternoon. The report's still pending," Ed said, picking up a pen and jotting down another note on the pad before him. "I think we're going to have to be a little more forceful in our quest for answers. I'm going to talk to the district attorney and explain exactly what we're dealing with so that he'll have no surprises if something surfaces. I'll also see about getting a warrant to search the Bakers' residence. Since we can't confirm Michael Baker's claim, I think it's important to see if we can make any evidentiary connection between him and Richard. We need to see if we can rule him out as a suspect in Richard Smythe's death," he said, laying down his pen. "Let me get started on arranging what we discussed. I'll talk to you two later."

Chapter Nineteen

Ashley was sitting on the front porch step with the baby when Jack drove into the driveway that evening. The moment she saw him, she lifted their son's little hand in a wave.

Jack smiled at the sight, and the tension that had been riding him that day evaporated. Stepping out of the car, he headed up the walk, the formula he had promised to pick up in his hand. "Hi, babe," he said, dropping a kiss on her upturned face, while automatically reaching for his son. He held the baby to his chest, breathing in the sweet smell that was uniquely his.

"Hi," Ashley replied, unable to suppress a smile at the easy way her husband handled the baby. She looked at Jack's face, seeing the love that was etched there, but also noticing the strain about his eyes. "Rough day?"

Jack shrugged. "I've had better," he said, moving over to take a seat next to her on the step. The sun was already starting to go down and a slight cooling breeze filtered through the air. "How was yours?"

"All right."

Jack shifted the baby to a more comfortable position. "What time did Kayla leave this afternoon?"

"She only left a couple of hours ago."

"How was she?"

Ashley reached out to touch the baby's hand. "Good. At least a lot better than she was when I found her."

"Did she open up any more about what it was that got her so upset?"

"It's like we thought. Going into the house today was rough on her. A lot rougher than she anticipated. She wasn't prepared for it."

"She seemed okay when Ryan and I got here. At least she was in control of her emotions."

"Mm. I think she's going to give it a little more time before she tries to come back to the house again."

"That's probably best."

"Did you find out anything more about Richard's death?"

"Not much," Jack admitted. "We have more than a few people of interest, but nobody that the evidence is pointing to exclusively."

"What about the murder weapon? Did it show up anywhere yet?"

"It hasn't been reported," Jack replied, wanting to get off the subject of the investigation. While he knew Ashley had a keen interest in these type of things, he felt as if he had been living and breathing it since the night of the murder. He wanted the chance to unwind. Trying to get her mind off of the topic without hurting her feelings, he changed the subject. "What are you two doing outside?"

Ashley shrugged and leaned back so that she rested on her elbows. "John was getting restless so I thought some fresh air might do him some good."

Jack looked down at the baby that rested so contentedly in his arms. "It looks like you were right."

"Mm. Hopefully he'll sleep well tonight. The last few nights have been a little rough."

"I know. And you've been taking the brunt of it. If he gets up tonight, I'll take care of him."

"You have to get up early tomorrow," she reminded him. "Are you sure you can handle it? You know he never goes right back down to sleep. He seems to think that it's playtime in the early morning hours."

"I can handle it. Worst case, I'll take him downstairs and watch television with him."

She rolled her eyes. "Then you'll both end up sleeping on the couch," she said, thinking of the times in the past where she had come downstairs and found her husband sound asleep on the sofa, and their son sleeping on his chest.

"John doesn't seem to mind."

"No, I know he doesn't. To be honest, I think he enjoys sleeping that way. He can hear your heartbeat, and that always lulls him into a secure sleep. But that can't be too good for you. Especially when you're working on a case."

"Let me worry about what's good for me," he said, reaching over to kiss her.

"It's your call."

"That's right, it is. Right now we have something more pressing to discuss."

"What?"

"What we're going to have for dinner. I'm starving," he admitted.

She looked at him knowingly. "You didn't have lunch, did you?"

"There wasn't time."

She sighed. "Sometimes I don't know what to do with you."

Jack ignored her words. "So what sounds good to you? I know you said to bring a pizza, but I thought if you still wanted that, we could just have it delivered. If you want something else, I'm game."

"Like what?"

"It doesn't really matter. Whatever you want is fine. We could even go to a restaurant if you want."

Ashley looked down at John who had fallen asleep on her husband's shoulder. "With John? Don't you remember the last time we took him to a restaurant? You had to eat your dinner with him sitting on your lap."

"So?"

"So, that's no way to enjoy your meal. Why don't we forget about eating out and grill something here? I can take some steaks out of the freezer and defrost them in the microwave."

"Sounds good to me," Jack said, relieved that they would be staying in. Ashley was right about one thing. It wasn't easy going to a restaurant with a baby. And more importantly, it wasn't even relaxing to him when he was working on a case. He always felt guilty about taking the time away from the investigation. He always felt as if he should be doing more to solve whatever case he was working on.

"Then that's what we'll do," she said, sitting upright and reaching for the baby. "Here, I'll take him."

"I got him," Jack said, ignoring her outstretched hands and rising to his feet.

"If we're lucky, he'll sleep for over an hour. We may just be able to fit dinner into his nap time."

"I'll put him in his crib. Are the blinds drawn?"

"Yeah, and the central air was on all day, so it should be nice and cool in there," Ashley said.

"Then we may just be in luck," Jack said, letting Ashley open the front door before he stepped through the threshold.

"When you take him up, make sure the baby monitor is on. I have the receiver already in the kitchen."

"Sure. Do I have time for a quick shower?"

"No problem. I'll put the steaks into the microwave to defrost and get the potatoes ready while you're doing that."

"All right. Don't worry about the grill though. I'll take care of that when I'm done," he told her.

Ashley nodded and watched while her husband walked toward the staircase, his hand absently rubbing John's small back. "Do you want me to come and help you get him settled?"

"Nah. We'll be fine," Jack said.

"Okay. Just speak into the monitor if you need me for anything. I'll go into the kitchen and get everything started."

"You got it."

Chapter Twenty

In the early morning hours, Jack was awakened from a sound sleep by the cry of his son. Opening his eyes, he lay in bed for a moment, trying to determine if it was a single, isolated cry, or if John was demanding attention. It didn't take him long to determine that it was the latter.

Jack automatically looked across at Ashley, noticing that she didn't stir. It was a strong indication of just how exhausted she was. Remembering his promise to her earlier, he rubbed a tired hand across his eyes before swinging his legs to the floor so that he could attend to John.

The small night-lights that Ashley had put throughout all the rooms illuminated his way through the darkened house. As he stepped through the doorway to his son's room, he immediately saw John's active movements that assured him that he was indeed wide awake.

"Hey," Jack said softly as he reached down and

163

picked him up. "We're going to have to have a talk about your sleeping habits one day."

John seemed unconcerned by his father's comments.

Jack shifted the baby to a more comfortable position and walked out of the bedroom to go downstairs to get a bottle. "Are you hungry?" he asked as headed toward the kitchen.

It barely took any time to fix the bottle and warm it, and it wasn't long before Jack was walking into the living room, his son safely held in the crook of his arm while he drank greedily from the bottle. Jack was just passing by the bay window on his way to the sofa when he caught sight of a flash of light from the corner of his eye. He paused, and turned his attention outside to the direction the light had come from, Kayla and Richard's house.

He stared across at the dark residence, his gaze automatically taking in the outside grounds. There were no cars in the driveway, nor any parked on the street in front of any houses within his sight range. At least none that didn't belong. Wondering if perhaps he had imagined the beam of light, he was about to turn away when he noticed it again. There was no mistaking it this time. There was someone inside the Smythe residence.

Jack tensed at the realization, which disturbed his son. Feeling the restless movements of the baby, he set about quieting him down while quickly turning and heading up the stairs to where Ashley was.

Ashley was still sound asleep when he entered the bedroom. "Ashley," Jack called, hating to wake her, but knowing he had no option.

When she didn't immediately answer, he called her

again. "Ashley," he said, his tone of voice expressing his urgency.

Ashley groggily opened her eyes. "What? What's the matter? What happened?" she asked with a hint of panic. There was only one reason she could think of for Jack to wake her, and that was if something was wrong with John.

"Somebody's in the Smythes' house. Take the baby. I'm going to go check it out," Jack told her.

"What?" Ashley asked, trying to make sense of his words now that she knew the baby was okay. She automatically reached for her son, holding him protectively to her chest.

Jack quickly put a shirt on before reaching for his gun. "Call the precinct and have them send a car out here now. Tell them to hold the sirens," he ordered, heading out the door.

As Jack stepped outside into the dark night, his senses went into heightened alert. He wasn't sure what he was about to walk in on. Common sense told him that the house could be getting burglarized because it was empty. Though they hadn't had that problem in the neighborhood in the past, it wasn't something the area was immune from. But there was some inkling in the back of his mind, some sixth sense that told him the person in the house at this moment might have had something to do with Richard's death.

Quickly crossing the street, he tried to be as quiet as possible. He didn't want to alert the intruder to his presence. He couldn't afford not to have the upper hand.

Cautiously, he made his way up the driveway, when

a thought occurred to him. The flashes of light he had seen earlier were in different parts of the house. The first was from the living room, the second from the bathroom window. If he followed the sequence of where he saw the lights, the person in the house was making their way toward the bedroom. Or rather, they were probably there by now.

Instead of taking the obvious route through the front door, Jack decided to go in through the backyard. He remembered that the wood fence that secured the perimeter of the property had a gate by the garage. Walking over to it, he inspected the latch. It was old and rusty, which meant that there was a good chance that it would make some noise when opened— something he couldn't afford. Deciding that the only way to avoid having the gate make any sound was to go over it, he quickly scaled it, landing in the backyard with barely a thump.

With his back to the house, he edged against the wall, his gun poised and ready to fire, while adrenaline pumped through his body as he mentally prepared to confront the intruder. As he got closer to the French doors that led to the master bedroom, he heard a creaking sound coming from that area. He paused, his eyes looking toward the direction of the sound.

Searching the darkness, he saw a shadowy figure step out of the doorway and one thought struck him: The security light that had gone on so quickly the night of the murder didn't register any movement. Though it had picked up his presence that night, the light wasn't on now.

He thought back, recalling that when he had stepped out of the bedroom onto the small patio, his stride had been long and straight, and he had triggered the sensor of the light fixture almost immediately. But the figure that stood on the patio now was moving in a different path. The person was within inches of the house's back wall and they were moving off to the side. The walking pattern was different than Jack's had been, the steps more of a shuffle than a stride. And the motion detector wasn't sensing the walker's range. It wasn't picking up the movement. It wasn't set to pick up the movement.

The reality that they had somehow missed the setting on the light the night of the murder hit Jack hard, but he didn't waste much time pondering the would have, could have, should have of the situation. All of his concentration was on the figure before him.

It was obvious that the person before him was familiar with the layout of the property and the security measures that were in place. The person was too careful in keeping their own back to the wall, too conscious about alerting anybody to their presence.

Jack watched from his vantage point as the dark figure stopped by the gutter downspout. From the distance of where he stood, he couldn't make out much of the person's build, other than it didn't seem to fit the description Kayla had given them the night of Richard's murder. It was much slighter than she had described. But dressed all in black with a dark ski cap hiding their hair, the darkness and the shadows camouflaged the person's identity.

When the person crouched with their back to the wall and reached a hand inside the gutter downspout, Jack decided to make his move. Stepping away from the house, he raised his gun. "Police! Freeze!"

The dark figure froze, and Jack quickly made his

way over to the patio. The moment he stepped in front of the French doors, the security light sensor registered his movement and activated the light, allowing him to get his first real glimpse of the intruder. It was Kayla Smythe.

Kayla held up a hand to shield her eyes from the harsh glare of the light.

"Step away from the spout, Kayla," Jack ordered, his full attention on the woman that stood before him. There was only one explanation for her to go to such lengths to keep herself from being seen coming back to the house in the middle of the night, with only a flashlight to guide her. And that was if there was something here that she didn't want to be associated with. If there was something here that she was trying to get out of the house undetected. Something that the search team had missed the night of Richard's murder.

"Jack . . ."

"I'm not going to repeat myself. Step back."

Kayla heard the command in his voice, and did as he instructed, while watching with something close to panic as Jack walked up to the spout. "Jack, I can explain."

Jack ignored her. Keeping his eyes trained on her, he reached into the opening of the spout. It was the flexible type, designed for easy movement. Made with the latest technology, it allowed the user to deflect the water to the area they wanted, away from any type of foundation. It was something that he and Ashley had incorporated into their own home.

As his hand negotiated the opening, he felt the cold touch of metal. He carefully gripped the object and pulled it from the tight space, realizing as soon as he cleared it from its confinement that he held the murder weapon. A small, sub-compact pistol.

Careful to not touch the grip, he stood to his feet. "You wanted to explain. I'm listening."

"It's not mine," she quickly denied, her face paling as she saw the weapon that he held.

"Isn't it?"

"No!"

"Then who does it belong to? Michael? Lois?"

"They didn't have anything to do with Richard's murder! I told you that."

"That's right, you did. A couple of times. But if they didn't do it, if you aren't protecting them, that leaves only you as the person who hid the weapon. And there would be only one reason for you to do that—you killed Richard."

She didn't say anything in response to his comment.

Jack saw the panic flare in her eyes, no longer protected by the night. He watched her body tense, and he could hear her breathing change, as the full reality of her situation hit her. And it was then that he knew, without any doubt, that she was the one who killed her husband. "You did, didn't you? You shot Richard. And the gun is the reason you came back to the house yesterday. You came back to get it. What happened, Kayla? Why didn't you take care of this yesterday when you had the chance? Did you have a tinge of conscience? Did the reality of what you actually did hit you? Did you suddenly realize that you had killed Richard in cold blood?"

She shook her head at the barrage of words, denying the charges. "You're wrong, Jack."

"Am I? Then explain to me what happened. Explain

what you're doing here tonight, sneaking around like a thief. Explain why you seemed to know exactly where the murder weapon was hidden."

She didn't speak.

"Talk to me, Kayla," he urged, sensing that she was going through an inner struggle. He could tell by her eye movements, by her body language, that part of her wanted to talk. Part of her wanted to clear her conscience, to alleviate the torment that she was living with. But he also knew that there was a more cold-blooded side to her nature. The side of her that had shot her husband and hid the gun without a moment's thought. The side that had tried to deflect suspicion away from herself by fabricating that she had seen an intruder kill Richard.

She continued to look at him silently, and he could tell that her mind was going a mile a minute, trying to determine what to do. Aware that she could go either way, that she could cooperate or hold her silence, he chose his next words with care. "Kayla, I can help you if you let me. I know you loved Richard. I know the anguish you're feeling. I know you didn't mean to kill him."

"I didn't," she whispered, her voice tortured.

"Then tell me what happened."

She held his gaze, not speaking.

"Kayla, I can help you if you let me," he repeated, trying to coax her out of her silence. "Talk to me," he beseeched, maintaining eye contact with her, willing her to trust him, trying to give her the time she needed to come to terms with the fact that the charade was over, that there was nothing left for her to do except explain the truth about what happened the night of

Richard's murder. It seemed like an eternity before she gave the briefest of nods.

Jack repressed the sense of relief he felt at her acknowledgment. Wanting to get her out of the backyard, away from any possible eavesdroppers, he stepped back and motioned her inside. "Let's go in," he said, waiting for her to precede him into the bedroom. He automatically reached for the light switch as he walked through the entryway.

The moment the light illuminated the area, Kayla froze, and an expression of pure torment crossed over her features.

Jack frowned and looked over at the area that held her attention. It was the spot where Richard's body was discovered. The bloodstains were still visible on the carpet, and the chalk outline stood out prominently on the dark fibers. "Kayla . . ." Jack prompted when she continued to stare transfixed at the area.

She turned to look at him, her eyes shimmering with unshed tears. "I loved Richard."

Jack didn't respond to the comment. There was nothing for him to say.

At his silence, the tears that had been building in her eyes began to flow. "You have to understand. What happened that night wasn't meant to happen."

"I'm willing to listen to whatever you want to tell me," he assured her, keeping his voice low and soft in an effort to encourage her to speak. Right now, at this moment, the most important thing was to find out what had occurred that night. He would sort through the rest later. He would make sense of everything after he got the facts.

"Jack . . ."

Thinking that she was about to stall, he felt compelled to point out, "You hid a gun, Kayla. Ballistics will be able to confirm that the gun you came to get tonight was the one you used to kill Richard."

"But you don't understand . . ."

"Then explain it to me."

"The gun wasn't mine. It was Richard's," she sobbed.

Chapter Twenty-one

"The gun was Richard's," he repeated, unsure of what to make from the remark.

"Yes," she answered, her voice breaking as she revealed the secret that she had been harboring. The one that tortured her night and day. "Except he never told me that he bought it. I found it the day of the block party in his bedroom while I was putting away some laundry."

Jack steeled himself against her emotional state. "So you took it?" he asked, trying to make sense of what she was telling him.

She reached up and wiped away her tears. "I hated guns. Richard knew I hated guns. I never wanted one in the house. Richard knew how I felt."

Her words didn't answer his question. "If you hated guns so much, why did you take it? Why not just ask him why he had it?" he asked, his only priority at the moment to get to the bottom of what had happened.

Her tears, which flowed so freely, no longer moved him. His concern now was for the truth.

Kayla trembled uncontrollably and moved over to the edge of the bed. Keeping her gaze averted from the spot where Richard had fallen, she tried to answer Jack's question, to explain how the tragedy of her husband's murder had occurred. She knew she needed to somehow get across that she hadn't meant to kill Richard. That what happened that night wasn't supposed to have happened. "I don't know why I took it. I was so angry when I found it. Richard always wanted to get a gun. He thought we should have one as protection. But I hated them. I always have. They terrified me," she confessed, looking at Jack, her eyes begging him to understand.

"Why?" he asked, having a hard time making the connection between her words and her actions on the night of Richard's murder.

"When I was younger and living on my own, I went home one night and I walked into an armed robbery."

"Were you hurt?"

"Emotionally. Psychologically," she said softly, her voice waning.

"Did Richard know about what happened to you?" Jack asked, trying to keep her talking so that he could get a complete picture of her mindset and what had transpired that led to her husband's murder.

She nodded slightly, her eyes closing briefly in anguish. "He did. And I think that's why I felt so betrayed when I discovered the gun. Richard was always talking about getting one, and I was constantly telling him that I didn't want one in the house. It was one of the things we fought about. It was the original reason that Richard had a separate bedroom."

"What do you mean?"

"Richard had gone to a gun show with a co-worker a few months ago. He came home and asked if I would mind if he purchased one. I told him I didn't want one in the house. He got upset and said that I didn't have the right to tell him what to do. He slept in a different room that night."

"And never moved back."

"Yes. The next night, he came home late from work and rather than wake me, he slept in the other room again. It soon became a habit."

"Did Richard ever mention getting a gun again?"

"No. So, I thought he understood my feelings. I thought he respected them."

Jack considered what she had just revealed. It explained a lot. He thought back to Ashley's comment about Kayla being tense the day before the murder when she was closing the basement windows. Jack now understood why. Kayla had experienced having her space violated. Her privacy. He knew that was something nobody ever recovered fully from. But she still hadn't explained why she took the gun from where Richard had kept it. If she truly hated them, that action didn't make sense. "Why did you take the gun when you found it?" he asked again.

Kayla ran a shaky hand through her hair. "I don't know. I just did. Like I said, I was angry that Richard had it."

Jack realized that her words were as much of an explanation as he would get. At least for now. Deciding to change tactics, he pressed on. "Did you mention the gun to Richard before the block party?"

"No. Richard was out of the house when I discovered it. He had gone to buy ice. By the time he returned, the party had started. I was already outside with the neighbors. I thought I would talk to him that night, after it was done. But I didn't get the chance. When Richard came in to make his business call, he discovered that the gun was missing. He went looking for it."

"And he found it," Jack concluded.

"Yes," she said on a shuddering breath. "When I came in to get Richard that night, I didn't see him. But I heard him in the bedroom. When I went back to get him, he was sitting on the side of the bed holding the gun. He looked at me when I walked in. He asked me what I was doing with the gun. I told him that I should be the one asking him that question. He got angry. He said that I should be grateful that he had bought it. Especially after claiming to have heard someone in the basement that morning. He said with my active imagination, it just made sense to have it. That it was his concern for me that caused him to get it, and that we were lucky that he was able to make contact with a man who was selling it. I argued that he had no right to get it without talking to me."

Jack was silent while she spoke, allowing her the time she needed to gather her thoughts and to tell him the sequence of events that occurred the night of Richard's murder.

"Things escalated from there," she continued. "He said he was taking the gun back to the room he was using, and that it was staying in the house. I don't know what happened then. All I know is that I didn't want it in the house. I reached for the gun and we struggled over it. It fired. Richard fell immediately." She looked at him with tormented eyes. "It was an accident, Jack. I swear to you. I never meant to kill Richard," she cried desperately.

There was an element in her voice that made him believe her. The devastation she was feeling was obvious. But there was still too much that was left unexplained. Like why she went out of her way to hide the gun. And why she gave the police a false description of an intruder. The sketch their artist had done, the way she described Richard's murderer, all pointed to premeditation.

"Why didn't you tell me what happened that night, Kayla? Why did you hide the gun? Why did you fabricate an intruder?" he asked.

"I panicked, plain and simple," she told him, her voice thick with tears and emotion. "I didn't know what to do. It didn't seem real. Richard was on the floor, his chest was covered with blood, and I had the gun in my hand. It all seemed so surreal."

Her voice trailed off after the last word, and Jack waited patiently for her to speak again.

"I knew he was dead. He wasn't moving. He wasn't breathing. I couldn't believe what had happened."

"Why did you hide the gun?" he repeated, pressing her for an answer.

"I don't know! I know that sounds like a lie, but it's the truth. I wasn't thinking rationally. When I stepped back from Richard, all I could look at was the gun in my hand. Every reason that I never wanted one in the house was lying there before me in black and white. I just wanted to get rid of it, to pretend that none of this had happened. I saw the downspout outside and I acted. Richard had made such a commotion when we installed it. Of how easy it was to maneuver away from the concrete, how flexible it was. I didn't think at that point. It was my first instinct to hide the gun. I think I was convinced that if I didn't have the gun on me, then I wasn't responsible for Richard's death. So I shoved the gun into the spout. I don't remember much after that. All I know is that I wanted to run. I wanted to hide."

"And that's how you ended up in the closet," he concluded, the pieces of the puzzle finally fitting together.

"Yes. It seemed like a safe place at the time. But the darkness kept closing in on me, and I couldn't get the image out of my mind of Richard's blood. I swear I didn't mean to kill Richard."

Jack didn't respond to her statement, he couldn't. His job demanded that he remain impartial. And there were still a lot of questions that needed to be answered. "Why did you come back here tonight? Why didn't you take the gun yesterday when you had the chance?"

"I tried. But I couldn't face this room in the daylight. Everything was too vivid," she whispered, her eyes going once more to the bloodstained carpet. "I keep reliving that night in my mind. I keep seeing the look in Richard's eyes as the gun fired. I thought if I came back in the darkness, I could exorcise the ghosts. I thought if I got rid of the gun, I might be able to face coming back into the house. I was wrong," she said, her voice a whisper.

Jack sensed that some of her anguish was being alleviated by the confession she just gave. And in a way, he understood that. Carrying that type of guilt around took its toll on all but the most hardened of hearts.

His attention was momentarily diverted by the slamming of a car door, and he knew that the backup he had instructed Ashley to call in had arrived. Now came the hard part. Kayla would have to repeat her story formally down at the station. Something he was sure that her family would fight. "Kayla, police officers are outside," he said, watching her closely.

She showed no reaction to his words.

"Kayla . . ." he prompted.

The sound of his voice penetrated through to her, and she glanced up at him without really seeing him.

Jack frowned at her vacant stare. "It's time to go down to the police station," he told her, wanting some sort of acknowledgment from her that she understood what he was saying.

She nodded.

Jack was a little worried by her silence. She seemed to withdraw fully into herself, distancing herself from reality. "You'll be able to call your sister from there," he said, hoping for some sort of response.

Still she didn't say anything.

Jack reached out to take her arm, helping her up from the bed. "I'll walk you out to the patrol car," he said, keeping a close eye on her as he felt her tremble beneath his touch.

A car pulled up to the curb as Jack assisted Kayla into the back of a waiting patrol car. He glanced in its direction, recognizing Ryan.

Ryan stepped out of his vehicle and waited until Jack had the woman safely ensconced inside the car before he walked over. "What's going on?" he asked after seeing the identity of the person. "I got a call that said Ashley had phoned the station to report an intruder at the Smythe residence."

Jack reached up a hand to rub away the tension in his neck. "Kayla just confessed to killing her husband."

"What?" Ryan asked, his voice betraying his surprise at the revelation.

"I found her in the backyard trying to retrieve the gun."

Ryan glanced at Kayla. He saw the open devastation in her expression. "Was it premeditated?"

"I don't think so. She says it was an accident, and I believe her."

"Was the gun hers?"

"She claims it was Richard's. It's a long story, but apparently Richard had somehow obtained a gun awhile back, after Kayla refused to have one in the house. She found it the day of the block party and moved it. When she came in that night, Richard had it in his hand. They argued about keeping it, and they were both trying to take possession of it. That's when it fired."

"But I don't understand. If it was an accident, why did she hide the weapon? Why did she fabricate an intruder?"

"She said it was her first instinct. She acted impulsively, without thinking. She was frightened."

"But our team searched the property," Ryan said, not understanding how the gun was overlooked.

"The gun was in the gutter downspout. Our suspicions were focused on the open window in the basement and the perimeter of the yard in that area. My guess is that nobody thought to search the drainage areas, especially the one by the master bedroom. I don't think anybody considered that the murder weapon was a sub-compact."

Ryan considered Jack's words. After a moment, he said, "Richard must have opened the window in the basement the day of the block party."

"Yeah," Jack agreed. "Ashley had made the comment that Kayla mentioned he liked them open. He must have been responsible for the thump she heard."

"But why wouldn't he have admitted that? Kayla said he just shrugged the whole thing off as if she imagined it," Ryan reminded him.

"Who knows. Maybe it was just his way of making sure that he was in control," Jack said, looking around at the police activity around him. "Where's Ed?"

"Down at the station talking to Carl Taylor."

"They picked him up?" Jack asked, surprised by the revelation.

"He showed up on his own. His mother made contact with him and talked him into coming down to talk to us. I think she understood the severity of the situation and convinced him that if he was truly innocent in Richard's murder, he needed to meet with us and clear things up."

"Sounds like a woman of sense," Jack said looking across the street to his own house and catching sight of Ashley staring out at him from the bedroom window. He lifted a hand in greeting and motioned silently to the patrol car, communicating that he would be going to the police station. He smiled slightly when he saw her wave, acknowledging that she understood. He turned his attention back to Ryan. "I want to be at the station when they process Kayla."

"So do I. I'll drive you and give you a lift back home later," Ryan offered.

"Thanks. Let me just brief the officers that are going to be securing the residence," Jack told him.

"Sure. While you're doing that, I'll call Ed and fill him in with what's going on," Ryan said, reaching for his cell phone.

"Okay," Jack said, walking away to talk to the officers. It was several minutes later before he returned to Ryan's side.

"All set?" Ryan asked.

"All set," Jack replied, giving the signal to the officer who would be driving Kayla to the station that they were getting ready to go. He turned to Ryan. "Did you reach Ed?"

"Yeah. He'll be waiting for us."

"Then let's go put this case to bed."